Dead Certain

"Jesus Christ," said Carter.

"It's Savine," Hobbs growled, playing his light across the body.

Lupat Savine was bound to a chair with wire around his legs and chest. He was naked, and there wasn't much of his body that hadn't been discolored from blows or cigarette burns. There was a pool of dried blood beneath the table from his wounds. The coup de grace had been delivered with a powerful pistol from short range. The hole in the front of his head was small and neat. The back of his head was all over the wall.

"You think he talked?" Hobbs asked.

"I'd bet the ranch on it," Carter said.

NICK CARTER IS IT!

"Nick Carter out-Bonds James Bond."
—Buffalo Evening News

"Nick Carter is America's #1 espionage agent."
—Variety

"Nick Carter is razor-sharp suspense."
—King Features

"Nick Carter has attracted an army of addicted readers ... the books are fast, have plenty of action and just the right degree of sex ... Nick Carter is the American James Bond, suave, sophisticated, a killer with both the ladies and the enemy."
—The New York Times

FROM THE NICK CARTER
KILLMASTER SERIES

AFGHAN INTERCEPT

THE ALGARVE AFFAIR

THE ANDROPOV FILE

ARMS OF VENGEANCE

THE ASSASSIN CONVENTION

ASSIGNMENT: RIO

THE BERLIN TARGET

BLACK SEA BLOODBATH

BLOOD OF THE FALCON

BLOOD OF THE SCIMITAR

BLOOD RAID

BLOOD ULTIMATUM

BLOODTRAIL TO MECCA

THE BLUE ICE AFFAIR

BOLIVIAN HEAT

THE BUDAPEST RUN

CARIBBEAN COUP

CIRCLE OF SCORPIONS

CODE NAME COBRA

COUNTDOWN TO ARMAGEDDON

CROSSFIRE RED

THE CYCLOPS CONSPIRACY

DAY OF THE ASSASSIN

DAY OF THE MAHDI

THE DEADLY DIVA

THE DEATH DEALER

DEATH HAND PLAY

DEATH ISLAND

DEATH ORBIT

DEATH SQUAD

THE DEATH STAR AFFAIR

DEATHSTRIKE

DEEP SEA DEATH

DRAGONFIRE

THE DUBROVNIK MASSACRE

EAST OF HELL

THE EXECUTION EXCHANGE

THE GOLDEN BULL

HELL-BOUND EXPRESS

HOLIDAY IN HELL

HOLY WAR

HONG KONG HIT

INVITATION TO DEATH

ISLE OF BLOOD

KILLING GAMES

THE KILLING GROUND

THE KOREAN KILL

THE KREMLIN KILL

LAST FLIGHT TO MOSCOW

THE LAST SAMURAI

LAW OF THE LION

LETHAL PREY

THE MACAO MASSACRE

THE MASTER ASSASSIN

THE MAYAN CONNECTION

MERCENARY MOUNTAIN

MIDDLE EAST MASSACRE

NIGHT OF THE CONDOR

NIGHT OF THE WARHEADS

THE NORMANDY CODE

NORWEGIAN TYPHOON

OPERATION PETROGRAD

OPERATION SHARKBITE

THE PARISIAN AFFAIR

THE POSEIDON TARGET

PRESSURE POINT

PURSUIT OF THE EAGLE

THE RANGOON MAN

THE REDOLMO AFFAIR

REICH FOUR

RETREAT FOR DEATH

THE SAMURAI KILL

SANCTION TO SLAUGHTER

SAN JUAN INFERNO

THE SATAN TRAP

SIGN OF THE COBRA

SLAUGHTER DAY

SOLAR MENACE

THE STRONTIUM CODE

THE SUICIDE SEAT

TARGET RED STAR

THE TARLOV CIPHER

TERMS OF VENGEANCE

THE TERROR CODE

TERROR TIMES TWO

TIME CLOCK OF DEATH

TRIPLE CROSS

TUNNEL FOR TRAITORS

TURKISH BLOODBATH

THE VENGEANCE GAME

WAR FROM THE CLOUDS

WHITE DEATH

THE YUKON TARGET

ZERO-HOUR STRIKE FORCE

ISLE OF BLOOD

KILL MASTER
NICK CARTER

JOVE BOOKS, NEW YORK

KILLMASTER #257: ISLE OF BLOOD

A Jove Book/published by arrangement with
The Condé Nast Publications, Inc.

PRINTING HISTORY
Jove edition/January 1990

ISBN: 0-515-10217-2

Jove Books are published by The Berkley Publishing Group,
200 Madison Avenue, New York, New York 10016.
The name "JOVE" and the "J" logo
are trademarks belonging to Jove Publications, Inc.

PRINTED IN THE UNITED STATES OF AMERICA

10   9   8   7   6   5   4   3   2   1

*Dedicated to the men and women of the
Secret Services of the
United States of America*

ONE

It was one of those sharp, clear, early-summer days that take away inhibitions, soothe taut nerves, and make one realize that if there were no people, the world would be a beautiful place.

The woman rose from the sand, yawned, and stretched her arms. Absently, she scratched her smooth dark stomach. Then, jiggling softly in her bikini, she walked to the water and gingerly stepped in. She sucked in her breath as a small roller washed across her knees.

Twenty yards behind her, relaxing on a chaise, Nick Carter grinned. The woman could suck in her breath with great effect.

She bent over. Her back glistened with oil as she slapped water over her body. She walked farther out until she was thigh-deep in the water and shivered, wiggling her rear end.

Her face turned toward Carter and the tip of her tongue came out and traveled along her lower lip. She knew exactly what she was doing.

"Aren't you coming in?"

"I'd rather watch," Carter replied.

She laughed and dived, submerging for a moment and then surfacing, her arms rolling in a smooth crawl.

Carter watched her for a moment and then shifted his eyes to the left. To the left was the beautiful resort of Izmir, tucked into its own bay on Turkey's Aegean coast. To the right, the tree-studded coastline stretched north in green splendor.

It was an idyllic spot. They had been there for five days. He could easily have taken another week.

But that wasn't to be, and Carter knew it. As if in answer to his thoughts, the telephone rang in the bungalow behind him.

He turned and jogged up the sand. The bungalow was isolated, standing in a grove of trees facing the wide, sandy beach. It had two bedrooms, a living room and kitchen, and a tiled terrace spread around the front affording a magnificent view of the sea.

Carter crossed the terrace into the living room and grabbed the phone. "Yeah?"

"We'll go tonight." It was the voice of Carl Hobbs, Carter's CIA liaison in Ankara.

"They've left?" Carter asked.

"All but a few flunkies closing the place up until they need it again."

"You've got the plans to the house?"

Hobbs chuckled. "There's a young clerk in the building administration office running around now on a brand-new Honda."

"Good work," Carter murmured. "What time?"

"I'll be there in a couple of hours. By the way, how's my secretary?"

"Fine," Carter replied, his eye wandering across the beach to where Reela Zahedi was emerging from the surf.

"I'll bet. See you in two hours."

Carter hung up and walked outside. Reela made quite a picture walking across the sand toward him. She was a very tall, very well built Amazon with handsome features, no makeup, and long black hair worn in two thick braids wound around her head.

About ten feet from Carter she unhooked the bikini's top

and let it slide down her arms. Her heavy breasts spilled from the skimpy garment, swaying delightfully as she moved.

"You have no shame," Carter said, his eyes glued on the large, dark areolas.

"No," she said, laughing, "but I have a lot of pride." She expanded her chest with a deep breath, finished wringing out the bra, and draped it across the back of a chair on the terrace.

"Carl called."

She moved into his arms until just the tips of her breasts touched his bare chest. "They have left?"

"Leaving," he replied, running his hand down her smooth back. "He got the plans to the house. We should be able to search it with a minimum of light."

"Is Carl coming out?"

Carter nodded. "He'll be here in about two hours."

She smiled and ran her hands down between their bodies to the swell in his trunks. "That's a long time."

She moved by him into the bedroom and Carter followed, catching her by the bed, turning her. They fell together and he molded his hands harshly over her breasts. The soft flesh filled his palms and her head thrashed from side to side.

"The rest of my suit," she moaned.

His hands slithered down over her ribs, over her taut belly, and on past the elastic of her bikini.

She arched again and he pulled the bottom of the suit down her legs. He stepped out of his own trunks and moved his body back up over hers.

He ran his lips down the valley between her taut, upthrusting breasts and then kissed her nipples until she began to tremble. Her flesh was cool and retained the salty tang of the sea.

Raising himself up, he crushed his mouth against hers, and when she felt the fullness of his probing strength, she caught her breath with a gasp and opened her thighs wider to welcome him. And then there was nothing but motion, hard thrusting muscle against soft yielding flesh, and while her head rolled from side to side, she moaned softly.

He lifted her hips up off the mattress and the fingers stroking his back became sharp claws as, suddenly, her body stiffened in his arms.

"Now," she moaned, thrusting upward and rolling herself until she was sitting on top of him.

She spread her legs for him again and slowly sat up, forcing him farther and farther inside her while her hands moved sensually up over her stomach until they cupped each breast with its firm pronounced nipple peeking between her fingers.

She began to move her hips with little bursts of aroused passion. Her eyes stared down into his. And then tantalizingly, teasingly, each time she undulated her hips, she lifted her body a little farther away from him until he grasped her thighs firmly, roughly, so that she couldn't escape completely.

"You're a witch," he whispered. "A sensual, wanton witch."

She laughed softly and sat down hard, until there was nothing separating them. She reached forward and caught hold of his chest with clawed fingers and her hips began to undulate once more.

As though sensing the passion she had aroused within him, her smile faded and her pelvic thrusts became violent, urgent. Carter lifted his loins and she ground her hips until suddenly her whole body stiffened in a frenzied climax and she rocked back, holding her stomach with her hands tightly. Her pelvic muscles contracted and Carter reared up in an orgasm that seemed to drain the air from his lungs.

Slowly, she collapsed over him.

Carter sipped coffee and went over the floor plan of the house for the tenth time since Carl Hobbs had arrived.

Hobbs lounged at the door, waiting for Carter to finish. He was taller and thinner than Carter, but of comparable age. Short dark hair curled over his ears. His skin was tanned a deep golden brown. The heavy lids drooping over his blue eyes lent them a melancholy weariness. His long girder of a jaw seemed to have fallen against his neck under its own weight. His nose was short and had wide nostrils. His lips bunched together as though he had fought against the habit of having his lower lip gape open. Fine hair covered the backs of his big hands and went down each finger almost to the nails. The sunlight made them shine like silver wire.

Carter glanced up from the plan and sensed the tenseness in the other man's body. "What is it, Carl?"

Hobbs shrugged. "Nothing, really. I just wish my man could have gotten around to the back and counted them as they came out."

"According to what Savine told Reela, they never leave a guard. The house is just used for meetings. When the meeting is over, they close it up until the next time."

Hobbs nodded with a growl and returned his attention to the sea. Carter turned his eyes back to the map, but his mind was on the situation.

He had gotten the assignment nearly three months earlier, and had busted his butt on it ever since.

Drago Vain was an Irishman, from Belfast. He had started his career twenty years earlier, when he was still a teenager, as an IRA bomber. But he didn't stop there. He went on to mass murder, bank robbery, and just about every form of terrorism imaginable.

He was as close to a wild-eyed maniac as a human could come. He had been sent to Libya and Lebanon for training, and graduated at the head of his class.

It had taken the British fifteen bloody years to find and

arrest Drago Vain. The general thinking was that the Irish revolutionaries were secretly glad to be rid of him. His indiscriminate killing was ruining them, public-relations-wise.

After two years in jail, Vain finally realized that no one was going to spring him. He escaped, made his way back to Northern Ireland, and took his revenge.

He dropped out of sight after that.

About a year ago, Interpol and almost every antiterrorist unit in the world got the word that a mercenary group had been put together that would do anything for the right price.

Drago Vain had gone into business, and instead of working for any cause now, he worked for hard cash.

By the time Carter got involved, Vain and his group seemed to be concentrating their efforts in Greece, Turkey, and the island of Cyprus.

Instructions from the head of AXE, David Hawk, had been clear and to the point: "Find out what this asshole is up to and end it."

Carter had dug, and had almost gotten himself killed twice in the process. Drago Vain played by no rules and he had no masters. If anyone got in his way, he terminated them.

Carter had enlisted Carl Hobbs and his CIA counterpart in Athens for help. It was Hobbs's beautiful assistant, Reela Zahedi, who had made the first break. She managed to turn one of Vain's lieutenants, Lupat Savine. From Savine they had learned that Vain's group was no longer for hire. They were going for much bigger things.

Vain, through intimidation and blackmail, had managed to get several Cypriot politicians under his thumb. He was also negotiating for a backer, one big enough to bankroll an enormous coup.

The question was, where?

And who had that kind of money?

The finalization of the plans was to take place at a safe

house that Vain kept in Izmir, Turkey. For a new identity and a lot of cash, Lupat Savine had agreed to tape the meeting and surreptitiously photograph the participants.

With that kind of information—and some luck—Carter was sure he could hold up the plan until he could get to Vain himself and terminate him.

A car stopped beside the bungalow and Carter saw Reela striding across the terrace. She had changed into a colorfully embroidered blouse with a low décolletage. One full sleeve had slipped down off a brown shoulder, and she was wearing a full skirt and her feet were bare. Her long black hair was braided again in two thick ropes and fastened at the end with ribbons. She looked like a peasant ready to go to market.

Remembering the days they had spent together, Carter wished they wouldn't need her that night.

But someone had to do the driving. The house was located in a residential area where a strange car parked too long in one place would arouse too much suspicion. Reela would have to drop them off, get out of the area, and return for them at a specified time.

She stepped into the room. "The car is all gassed, ready to go."

"Reela," Carter said, "run the business about Savine by me again."

She shook a cigarette from Carter's pack, lit it, and sat in the opposite chair.

"Like I told you, after our initial meet and agreement, everything had to go through his sister, Deemy."

"She's in Damascus?"

Reela nodded. "Sometimes I went there, sometimes she met me here in Turkey, in Antalya. The last time we met, Savine had told her to tell me about the meeting. Drago Vain had put a clamp on everyone in the inner circle. Until the meeting was over and the plan was in full operation, no one was to communicate with anyone outside the group."

"So Savine couldn't pass the tape and film to his sister."

"That's it. He told her he would leave it in the house, behind one of the radiators."

Carter ran a finger across the floor plan of the house. "Fifteen rooms, probably two radiators per room."

Carl Hobbs joined them at the table. "My God, Nick, what's the problem? If we're quiet and don't show any light, we'll have all the time in the world to hunt for the tape. Hell, all night."

Carter rubbed his chin. "I know."

"Then what's bothering you?" Reela asked.

"Drago Vain," Carter replied. "I've been living with this bastard for over two months. He's crazy and he's cunning. This business with Savine seems to be too easy, like it just dropped into our laps."

"Not so," Reela replied. "I did a lot of legwork to find the weak link, Lupat Savine. Let me tell you, Nick, the man is nothing but a thief, a cold-blooded killer who's been in most of the hellhole jails in the world. But he's afraid of Drago Vain. In Savine's own words, 'the Christians think the Antichrist will come. Believe me, he is here. I have seen him. He is called Drago Vain.' And while he was telling me that, Nick, this big mean bastard was shaking like a leaf."

Hobbs laid a hand on Carter's shoulder. "C'mon, my man, it's got to be done. Let's just do it."

Carter checked his watch. "All right. We'll leave right after dark."

TWO

Sir Jonas Avery flew commercial from London to Paris. He was accompanied by his usual entourage of two secretaries and a bodyguard.

The reason for the trip given to the media was a mundane conference between Sir Jonas and his French counterpart in the U.N. In fact, he was on the mission of his life. If it was successful, it would be the culmination of a twenty-year dream.

Sir Jonas was Her Majesty's representative to the U.N. He was known as a fair and brilliant negotiator. For the past five years he had been trying to bring together the Cypriot heads of the Turkish and Greek factions on the isle of Cyprus.

Since the island had achieved independence from Great Britain in 1960, there had been ill feeling and little or no negotiations between the two sides. In 1964 open fighting erupted until a U.N. peacekeeping force stepped in to negotiate a peace. This was done, but it was an uneasy truce, with the island separated much like East and West Germany.

Sir Jonas's dream was to unite the two sides and return the island to Cypriot rule, and do away with the barriers created by the Turkish and Greek governments.

Assim Kalvar and Nikos Proto were both Cypriots, natives of the island. Kalvar was a Turk, Proto a Greek, and

9

for as long as anyone could remember the two men had hated each other for that reason alone. Both were rebels, and neither of them held office. But both men held tremendous sway over their respective people on the island.

Proto was the head of the Greek-Cypriot party on Cyprus. He was an outlaw in exile somewhere on Crete, but that didn't diminish his power in his homeland. One word from Nikos Proto and his Greek followers would remove their guns from the hiding places of 1964 and start the war all over again.

Assim Kalvar was the equal power on the Turkish side of the U.N. line. He, like Proto, wanted a united Cyprus, but ruled by a government dominated by those of Turkish descent.

Until Sir Jonas took an active interest, there was a stalemate between the two men.

Through years of hard work, Sir Jonas had been able to finally bring the two men together. Most of the agreements had been reached. It needed now only a secret sit-down between the three men to formally sign the accord. Once this was done, steps could be taken to withdraw the U.N. force and a Cypriot government could be re-formed.

The meeting was scheduled to take place on neutral ground, in Nice, France, and that was the reason Sir Jonas had flown to Paris.

From Orly airport, the group was whisked to the Crillon by limousine. There, a suite and three adjoining rooms had been reserved.

Waiting for Sir Jonas in the suite was a prepacked bag and a gentleman from the Paris theater. The bag was full of off-the-rack and out-of-the-bin French clothes, the type of clothing a middle-of-the-road salesman would wear on vacation. The gentleman from the Paris theater was there to alter Sir Jonas's appearance.

Two hours later, the English diplomat was removed

from the hotel through a basement entrance. He was driven to a small village one hour north of Paris. There, his bodyguard reluctantly bid him farewell. The man knew Sir Jonas's mission was to be ultrasecret, but he disliked intensely the idea of turning the elderly man loose without a shred of security surrounding him.

An hour after his arrival in the village, Sir Jonas took a bus to Chartres. There, he booked a room in a small pension, using a French passport in the name of René Foulaurd.

The following morning he would board a train for Nice on the French Riviera.

Petro Canavos enjoyed his job. For the last four years he had lived the good life and traveled much of the world, free. He also made an excellent salary, much more than he ever dreamed he would make as the semieducated son of a Cypriot grape picker.

Canavos was the chauffeur and bodyguard of his boyhood hero, Nikos Proto.

It was a good life, especially when they would return to the villa that Proto maintained on the Greek island of Crete. On Crete there wasn't so much need for twenty-four-hour security. Petro could slip away one or two afternoons a week and rent a bungalow at the Olympia Hotel.

This afternoon, Petro had done just that. Now he was stretched out by the pool, glass in hand, surveying the latest crop of American and British tourists. They lined the poolside like a blanket of golden flesh.

He was finding it extremely difficult to make a choice, when a long-legged, high-breasted, dark-haired goddess blocked his light.

"Do you have a light?"

Petro smiled and rolled his bronzed, heavily muscled

body from the chaise. "For you, I would burn the hotel down just to light your cigarette."

"Just a little flame will do."

He lit her cigarette and one of his own. "Your Greek is good, but you are not Greek."

"French. I am Charmaine."

"I am Petro. Please, sit down. A drink?"

"What you're having is fine."

He poured another glass from the pitcher on the tray and she sat on the chaise beside him. "The French are lovely people."

"You are very kind. I myself find Greeks most attractive."

Ten minutes of chitchat and Petro knew he had scored. He ordered lunch for the two of them, and by the end of it, his eyes devouring the exquisite contours of her nearly bare body, he had only one thing in mind.

"I have an excellent brandy in my bungalow." Her voice was syrup.

Petro trailed her to her bungalow. Just inside the door, he whirled her into his arms and mashed his lips to hers. He was trying to free her breasts from her bikini top when she escaped his arms.

"A drink first, remember?" she chided coyly.

"Of course," he replied.

She moved into the tiny open kitchen. "Oh, no ice. I must have ice. Do you have any in your bungalow?" As she spoke, she slipped the bra from her shoulders and let it dangle from one hand at her side. "I'll get comfortable while you're gone," she breathed huskily.

Petro practically ran from her bungalow across the manicured lawn to his own. He unlocked the door and hurried to the small refrigerator.

"Damn," he cursed aloud as he tugged at the ice tray that seemed to be frozen in place. He tugged harder.

Then suddenly it released. Petro fell backward with his own momentum. But he never hit the floor, at least not in one piece.

The bungalow exploded with a thunderous roar. The picture window blew out and part of the roof fell in as flames shot skyward.

Petro Canavos never heard any of it.

Nikos Proto was a big man, with a powerful, work-toughened body, and severe, uncompromising features. His naturally dark skin was tanned even darker, not prettily from the sun but from exposure to all kinds of weather.

Proto was not the kind of man who sat behind a desk. He was a politician, yes, but he was a rebel first, a guerrilla fighter who loved to live in his mountains as well as fight in them.

He thought about this as he carefully packed his bag for Nice. The fighting would be over now. He trusted Sir Jonas Avery, and the Englishman had assured him that Kalvar had agreed to each and every one of his stipulations.

So now there would be peace. Proto growled a sigh. He would miss the good old days. He had given up sex many years before, and since that time the only thing he really enjoyed in life was killing Turks.

He snapped the bag shut, and suddenly froze.

Was that a sound from the first floor of the villa?

His hand crept up inside his jacket, to the inside pocket where he always carried the slender Beretta. With his other hand he checked the thin knife inside his belt.

He had released the maid for a week. Petro wasn't due back from his whore hunting for at least another two hours.

Could someone have scaled the wall and entered the house? Next to impossible with the alarm. And the dogs hadn't barked.

Nikos Proto's hands moved to fold themselves over his

stomach. They rested lightly, almost in a priestlike fashion, as he walked into the hall and down the stairs.

"Caryella, did you come back for something? Petro . . .?"

He paused at the bottom of the stairs, his hands ready, every sense alert.

He heard nothing.

Paranoid, he thought, even in Greece he was paranoid. Just when he was ready to sign a pact of peace with his enemy, he was paranoid.

He moved toward his office. He would have a glass of ouzo and relax until Petro returned to take him to the plane.

Nikos Proto was just inside the door when a heavy wooden statuette swung at him from nowhere. It crunched into his face, snapping bones in his nose and cheek.

Proto fell awkwardly against the wall and then slid to the floor, trying to maintain consciousness, gasping through a bloody mouth, spitting broken teeth. He looked up and tried to focus on the two men who stood over him, but he could not. He could see, however, that one now held an automatic pistol in a muscular left hand. The other man reached down and removed Proto's Beretta.

"Get up!" the second man said sharply to him in Greek.

Proto sat there for another moment, letting strength return. He tried to rise then and fell back to the floor. The room seemed to turn on an axis. He tried once more to get to his feet, and succeeded. He could focus better now, and saw that he was in trouble.

They were killers, pros, and no amount of talking was going to deter them from doing what they had been hired to do.

He had no choice. He would die, there was little doubt of it. But he would die like a man.

He went for the knife, freed it, and thrust toward the

nearest man. He heard a gasp of surprise and a growl of pain as he twisted and withdrew the blade for another thrust.

He saw the spurt of flame from the gun in the second man's hand. He tried to cry out, but felt only air rush from his mouth as his chest seemed to be smashed back into his spine.

Proto looked up as the man bent over him. "Why . . . who?"

The killer said nothing. He raised his revolver and fired another slug into Proto's chest.

The pain was all-consuming, searing, as though scalding steel was being poured into his body.

Proto had often wondered what the men he had shot felt like as they were dying.

Now he knew.

It was a trick, all a trick, he thought.

Kalvar, you bastard pig!

THREE

Reela Zahedi drove just under the speed limit, maneuvering the car like a slithering cat through the dense traffic. Carter sat beside her, with Carl Hobbs in the rear. All three of them had remained silent since leaving the bungalow.

The moon was high, glittering off the sea behind them and the whitewashed houses before them as they left the city and drove up into the hills.

"How much farther?" Carter asked, his voice almost a whisper.

"Not far," Reela replied, "maybe a mile."

"Still nervous?" Hobbs chuckled from the back seat.

"Screw you," Carter said without rancor, and pulled Wilhelmina, his 9mm Luger, from the shoulder rig under his left armpit. He checked the clip, jacked a shell into the chamber, and reholstered the piece.

In the back seat, he heard Hobbs doing the same with the modified Uzi he would carry into the house under his jacket.

Carter smiled.

Hobbs may not have doubts or be nervous about this little caper, but he was taking no chances.

"Just around the next corner," Reela said.

"Go past it," Carter ordered.

She made the turn and Carter's eyes searched the block.

It was quiet, peaceful, no streetlights and just a few lights
burning in the houses.

Drago Vain's safe house was big and ugly with almost
all its garden in the front.

Reela drove around the block twice. There was no light
anywhere in the target house.

"Looks good," Hobbs murmured.

"Yeah," Carter agreed, nodding, thinking that at any
time the people next door might get a sight of them in the
garden or working the front door lock, and Turkish police
would be all over them like flies on manure.

Reela pulled up at the end of the block. Hobbs was out
of the car and walking within a second, as if breaking into
dim suburban houses was all he lived for.

Carter squeezed Reela's thigh. "Take care."

He dived out and followed Hobbs. Reela made a U-
turn. She would park six blocks away and wait for them.

They moved along an alley and vaulted a low fence in
the rear. By the time Carter caught up with the CIA man,
Hobbs was already trying a ring of master keys in the rear
door.

Nothing moved.

"Dead bolts?" Carter asked.

Hobbs nodded.

If possible, they wanted no telltale signs of their entrance. That dealt out picks, and doing a window was out
of the question. They retreated to the rough stone wall and
edged toward the front.

Hobbs went up the stairs and studied the lock. "It's an
old Zeiss. I've got it." It took him sixty seconds to find a
key and he was in. Carter checked the street and adjoining
houses and followed.

They stood in the little square hall waiting for the darkness to soften, with no idea where the furniture was. The
front door was glass, and a long uncurtained hall window

ran along one wall high up. They couldn't use flashlights yet.

To Carter the place smelled wrong. He couldn't say what it was, but Hobbs seemed aware of it too. For a moment the two of them stood frozen under the window. Then Hobbs dropped to a crouch and, marvelously light and sure, moved forward. Carter heard a door open and Hobbs whispered, "Here."

It was a room off the hall but far darker. That meant lined curtains. Carter switched on his flashlight. As he did so, he realized that, apart from the carpets and curtains, he expected to find the house bare. In fact, as he raised the light beam slowly from the floor it lit up first a long heavy sideboard, then a grand piano, a large roll-top desk, and a low, expensive settee in suede.

"Desk?" Hobbs asked.

"No, they wouldn't be that careless or dumb. Just the radiators."

They moved from room to room on the first floor, thoroughly checking behind each of the radiators. Carter took one side of the main first-floor hallway, Hobbs the other.

Fifteen minutes later they met at the foot of the stairs.

"Anything?" Hobbs asked.

"A lot of dust. You?"

"The same. Let's go up."

They started at the rear and moved forward, Carter on one side, Hobbs on the other. In the second room Carter entered, he stopped short at the door.

Clothes had been thrown everywhere. The mattress and pillows had been pulled from the bed and opened with a sharp knife or razor. In the middle of the mess he spotted a wallet. It had been ripped open and turned inside out. Cards and snapshots had been tossed carelessly aside.

He took only a few seconds to check. The moment he spotted a Syrian identity card in the name of Lupat Savine, he scooped everything up and shoved it into his jacket pocket.

He was checking behind the radiator when he heard a hiss from the doorway behind him. "Nick, across the hall."

Carter moved behind the other man into a large bedroom fronting the house.

"Jesus Christ."

"It's Savine," Hobbs growled, playing his light across the body.

Lupat Savine was bound to a chair with wire around his legs and chest. Wire also bound his wrists together so tightly that it had disappeared into the flesh. He was naked, and there wasn't much of his body that hadn't been discolored from blows or cigarette burns. There was a pool of dried blood beneath the table from his wounds. The coup de grace had been delivered with a powerful pistol at short range. The hole in the front of his head was small and neat. The back of his head was all over the wall.

"You think he talked?" Hobbs asked.

"I'd bet the ranch on it," Carter said. "Look at him. No one could have held up under that treatment."

"I'm gonna check the radiators in the last two rooms anyway."

Hobbs moved off and Carter crouched by the front window. There was little doubt in his mind now. They had been set up.

Squinting, he checked the lawns and gardens of the adjoining houses and the street.

Then he saw it, slight movement in the big, tree-filled front garden. He couldn't be sure if it was one man or two. It seemed stupid for two of them to bunch and approach the house. Then he saw a third man standing without cover in a corner near the gate, out of the patch of moonlight but clear enough to be seen.

"Nothing," Hobbs said, coming back into the room.

"Get down!" Carter hissed. "It's a setup. I've already spotted three of them out there."

Hobbs dropped to his knees and took the other side of the window. "Shit."

"There must be a gaggle of 'em," Carter said, "or they wouldn't be bunching like that. They're probably all the way around the house, and when they move they could come from anywhere."

"Hell," Hobbs hissed, "they could even be inside, downstairs."

"Don't think so," Carter whispered. "We've been quiet. I think we would have heard them."

He chanced another look and evaluated their situation. He rejected getting alongside Hobbs and his Uzi and making a run through the back garden if it looked clear. The men in the front were too conspicuous. They were there to drive Carter and Hobbs out in the other direction, where they could be nailed away from the street.

"How many do you think?" Hobbs growled.

"Three as diversion, so at least seven."

"Too many," Hobbs reflected, as if this were disputed.

"What will they do?" Carter said.

"They'll come and get us. They've got to."

What was there to listen for? They would have a key, or they would break a window. Breathing. Feet on the stairs. A rush, and possibly some shots, and then it would be the end.

"I can cover the stairs," Hobbs said, slapping the Uzi. "They'll play hell getting up here through the fire this baby will lay down."

"Suicide shit," Carter breathed, peering out the window again.

"Better make up your mind," Hobbs said.

Carter looked. Three of them were walking toward the front door not even bothering with cover.

Anger welled inside Carter. He could feel it like a growth in his gut, a burning sourness in his stomach.

"Well, piss on waiting for 'em," Hobbs barked, and got to his feet.

Before Carter could stop him, Hobbs was firing burst after burst through the window. The three men fanned out at once, running crouched for the shadows.

One man screamed and did a gainer over the wall. A second one fell but struggled up in the grass and started to crawl with a leg hanging out slack behind him.

"Now!" Hobbs shouted, firing at the third. "Jump now, I'll cover you!"

Carter pulled himself up on the curtains, expecting return fire from below. There was no reason for them to remain quiet now.

Nothing came.

All he heard was the sound of running feet from the first floor. There was shouting and the crash of falling furniture.

Hobbs cleared the fragments of glass from the window-frame with the barrel of the Uzi.

"Go, for chrissake!" he roared. "I'll cover and follow you!"

The Uzi barked again and Carter rolled over the sill. He hit the tile roof on his backside and immediately started sliding with nothing to slow him down.

Above and behind him the firing stopped long enough for Hobbs to change magazines. Automatic fire crackled in the garden and, falling, Carter saw the bricks and wood and Hobbs's face spurt under the line of shots. Dust, splinters, and blood thickened the air, bounded on the roof above, as Carter hit the grass, somehow feet first.

He dropped and rolled. Stunned, he rolled the wrong way, toward the shed where two of them had taken cover, possibly three. Looking up at the window as he revolved on the sprouting ground, he glimpsed what used to be

Hobbs hanging down over the sill, his hair trailing, and blood splashing the ground and soaking the wall, running from his mouth and skull. There was someone standing behind him staring down into the garden.

Then there was firing from behind the shed and the windows of the house. They were shooting at shadows, but with the abundance of fire it was only a matter of time until they got him by accident.

Carter pressed his hands into the ground and hurled his legs back so he jackknifed away from his spot, hitting the ground again with his stretched-out right foot, his stronger leg always, and jerked toward the drive and the little front wall.

He saw dust and chips leap from the yellow brick gate-pillar, the same tearing breakup that he had witnessed under the window. The gun he had not heard. Zigzag was the order of the day and he did, gasping to get air into his straining lungs. He waited for the tiny high-explosive shells to be among his feet and legs and the rest of him, and then his knees struck the low wall and he fell forward over it into the street without damage.

Rolling back immediately, he cowered into the bottom of the wall, shielded for a moment from no matter what angle, and then crawled fast, down along the wall and away from the house, down the street.

He could hear all hell breaking loose behind him as he raced for the corner. Lights were coming on in every house now, and from somewhere he could hear the roar of an engine and the scream of tires.

He turned the corner at full tilt and practically ran right into two cars nosed together to block the street. At the same time he saw movement to his left and right and a man stood up between the cars in front of him.

He dived toward the ground. The brick wall behind him exploded with chips as the muzzle blast of a shotgun rolled over him. He hit and rolled, clawing the Luger into the open.

The man to his right had been surprised by Carter's sudden appearance. Now he was snatching at the inside of his jacket. The Killmaster squeezed off two rapid shots.

The man was slammed back against the car behind him. He slid to the ground as Carter spun, looking for the one to his left.

He was kneeling, leveling a pistol at Carter, and his lips were drawn back from his yellow teeth in a frozen expression of anger and fright. The pistol in his hand barked as Carter pulled the trigger. He felt a dull blow strike his left shoulder as the man was tossed backward. There was a small red mark on the kneeling man's throat that suddenly turned into a gushing stream of crimson. He dropped his pistol and fell to the sidewalk, his eyes wide and staring and a choked, gagging sound coming from his open mouth as he clutched his throat and kicked his feet.

Carter pushed himself up to a crouched position and ran along the side of the car by him. A window in the car suddenly caved in as the thunderous roar of the shotgun split the air again.

Carter dived behind the car, and another blast from the shotgun scorched the pavement by the rear wheel. He lifted his head and looked through the back window. The man was crouched down and trotting along the walk in front of the wall, moving toward him.

Carter dropped to his stomach and looked under the car. He saw the man's feet. He gripped the Luger harder and steadied it. He put the barrel on the center of the man's trouser leg and squeezed the trigger.

The Luger cracked sharply and jumped in his hand, and the man screamed hoarsely. He fell to the walk, the shotgun flying from his hands and rattling against the side of a car.

Carter jumped up and trotted around the car. The man was squirming toward the shotgun and reaching for it, a pool of blood forming under one of his feet. He looked up. Carter pointed the pistol and pulled the trigger. A tiny spot of red appeared on the man's forehead as his head snapped back, and the back of his head exploded, spraying blood and brains out onto the walk.

The engine roar he had heard earlier was louder now, a torrent of sound. Then the car screamed around a corner from the down side of the hill and its lights came hurtling directly at him.

Carter dropped to one knee and leveled the Luger.

Just in time, the car veered. The lights went to the side so he could see it was Reela's determined features behind the windshield.

She slammed the brakes and spun the wheel, broadsiding the car toward him.

Carter had the door open and was diving into the front seat while it was still moving.

"What happened?" she cried.

"We were set up," Carter shouted. "Move it!"

"Where's Carl?"

"He's dead."

"Oh no, oh my God, no . . ."

"Goddamnit, yes. He's dead, so we can't do anything about it. So move this iron!"

She was good. She forced her instincts to take over from her emotions and put her foot to the floor.

"Back to the bungalow?" she gasped.

"No," Carter growled. "They've probably got it pegged, too. Head up the coast. We've got to get the hell out of the country."

Minutes later the frozen lack of feeling in his shoulder was replaced by a throbbing, excruciating pain that sent tendrils of fire lancing through his entire left side. His left arm was numb and unresponsive. He could feel warm, sticky blood trickling down his arm and left side, and he felt nauseated and slightly light-headed. But the need to escape and get out of the vicinity was an imperative clamoring in his mind.

"Go left up there. Stay on the coast road."

"What then?"

"We'll find a fishing village. I've never met a Turkish fisherman yet who wouldn't take a bribe."

He unbuttoned his coat and cautiously pushed it off his left shoulder, wincing with pain. He turned on the courtesy light and looked at the wound. It was a crease, and the bullet had plowed through the skin and muscle tissue to a depth of a quarter of an inch at the deepest point. The sweater was stuck to his shoulder and arm with clotted and drying blood, and torn shreds of the sweater were in the wound. The bleeding had slowed, and it was painful, but not a cause for immediate alarm.

Reela glanced over and gasped. "You're hit!"

"I'll live," Carter said, laying his head back against the seat. "And you'd better slow down to the speed limit."

She did, and Carter fished in his pockets until he found a cigarette. He got one lit and they rode for several minutes in silence until Reela spoke.

"Did you find anything? In the house, I mean."

"Yeah. What was left of Lupat Savine."

FOUR

The hotel was not the worst in Antalya, but it was far from the best. But it was close to the airport, and that was a necessity.

Two men waited in a top-floor room. They had been waiting for three days. The larger man lay on one of the twin beds nearest the door. He lazily smoked a small cigar and stared at the ceiling. He was naked except for a pair of boxer shorts too large for his bulk.

The other man, younger and smaller, with dark eyes and coal-black hair that curled over his ears and forehead, sat cross-legged on the second bed. He was raptly watching an American television show that had been dubbed into Turkish.

"I wouldn't want to live in America," the younger man said.

"Oh?"

"No. It's so violent. Look at how they kill each other. Is that all they do in America? Kill each other?"

The bigger man blew a smoke ring. "Americans are violent people."

The telephone between the beds rang. Calmly, the big man swung his legs off the bed. He deliberately put out the cigar. After the third ring he picked up the phone. "Yes?"

"It is on," came the reply.

"All right."

27

"An envelope is at the front desk of your hotel."

"And the boat?"

"The *Madji*, pier four at Alanya. It will take you across to Kyrenia on Cyprus. Everything else is just as you were told."

The big man and the caller hung up simultaneously without another word.

"Well?" the slender man asked.

"It is on."

They dressed in dark, expensive silk suits, subdued shirts, carefully knotted neckties, dark socks, and custom-made Italian leather shoes.

With a last glance around the room, making sure nothing remained of their stay, they locked the door and took the elevator to the lobby.

While the big man stopped at the front desk and took a large envelope from the clerk, the younger man telephoned for a taxi. They waited inside. The sun had gone down, but the crushingly hot, humid air remained. The faces of people entering the lobby streamed sweat.

During the taxi ride to the airport, the big man opened the envelope. Inside he found two thick wads of money and a single sheet of paper. The typescript on the paper read: *BLACK SIMCA VAN—LICENSE JJL–94333. TIER 2, ROW A, SLOT 6.*

He put the money in his flight bag and, when he had memorized the information on the paper, rolled it into a tiny ball and pushed it out the window.

They got out in front of the terminal building, two well-dressed businessmen catching a flight. The younger man paid the cabbie, counting out a modest tip.

Side by side, they entered the terminal and walked the length of the lower floor to the exit leading to the parking ramps.

Finding the van was a simple matter. When they

reached it, both of them glanced around. It was clear. They each pulled on skintight surgical gloves, and the younger man retrieved the keys from a magnetic holder hidden under the rear bumper.

He opened the rear doors of the van. Inside was a long, rectangular black case. They climbed into the van, tossed their flight bags behind the seats, and opened the case.

Inside was a Czech Model 59 machine gun with a bipod, telescopic sight, and two one-hundred-round, non-disintegrating metallic link belts.

They both grunted their approval, and the younger man spoke. "Who is the hit anyway?"

"Do you care?"

"No."

"Then let's go do it," the big man said, slamming the trunk.

A truly classless society can be found only in the second-class compartments of French trains. All manner of humanity—rich and poor, ambitious and idle—come together on common ground for a few brief hours. Desiring this general anonymity, Sir Jonas Avery slid open the door to a compartment that contained four others besides himself.

As the disguised diplomat took his seat, he studied each of them in turn. He felt safe, but in his day he had seen enough violence and intrigue that he was never completely off guard.

One was a Spanish Gypsy with a wrinkled, nut-brown face and a gray stubble of beard. He talked incessantly, telling outrageous lies as the train rattled along.

A peasant woman was paying a visit to her sister in Avignon. She carried an enormous basket filled with bread, bottles of wine, sausage, and cheese, all of which she insisted on sharing.

A student was on his way to Cannes where he hoped to get a job on a yacht as a deckhand for the summer.

The fourth was a nun. Enveloped in her black robes with her white, starched cap and black headscarf, her white collar and with her face devoid of all makeup, she looked scrubbed, clean, and very pure. She wore heavy, ugly black shoes that protruded incongruously from under the hem of her habit. She was very quiet and shy but had a sweet smile that was breathtakingly beautiful in its innocence. She held a small, well-worn, leather-backed Bible open on her lap as though reading it, but her clear gray eyes watched everyone and she listened to them with almost breathless awe. Yet she became flushed and embarrassed when they tried to bring her into the conversation.

Sir Jonas's French was fluent and almost without a trace of accent, but he still kept his conversation to a minimum, feigning sleep.

The train rolled on. Passengers left and new ones got on. By the time they pulled out of Avignon on the last leg toward the Riviera and the sea, there was only Sir Jonas and the Gypsy in the compartment.

Then the compartment door slid open and a man entered. In a single, quickly comprehensive glance, Sir Jonas noted that he was short, opulently stout, with a full face in which a thin-lipped slash of a mouth seemed somehow out of place.

With a brief mumble that could have been taken for anything, the newcomer sat down in the far corner, away from the window and opposite Avery, and spread open a newspaper.

Sir Jonas glanced out the window as a small village flashed by the speeding express. He refocused his eyes, and saw in the reflection of the window that the man with the full-moon face had shifted his watery blue eyes from the newspaper and was studying him intently.

Too intently, Sir Jonas thought.

He felt the sudden, sharpened alertness of impending danger. Inside his shirt, under his belt, he had the small .22 automatic that his chauffeur-bodyguard had forced upon him. He resisted the impulse to move his hand toward it as he turned back from the window.

The man's attention had returned to the newspaper.

Avery's mind was glued to the other man. The unnatural tenseness in the stranger's body increased his wariness. Sir Jonas reached for his own newspaper, opened it, and behind its protective shield glanced again at the window. The moment lengthened as he kept his eyes fixed on the mirrorlike reflection. He became more conscious of the man's growing nervousness.

Twice the man's right hand moved slowly toward the inside pocket of his coat and then hesitated, stopped, and returned to the paper.

Sir Jonas kept his face expressionless while his nerves tightened. As though searching for a more comfortable position, he stretched and slid slightly along the hard leather seat. He crossed his legs and began slowly swinging one foot.

He waited, certain of what was to come. He might be making a hell of a mistake, he told himself, but he doubted it. He kept his eyes on those telltale fingers.

Suddenly the compartment door swung open. A redheaded woman of majestic proportions came through the opening like a galleon under full sail. The man jumped to his feet. Before he was steady, the woman landed a whacking open-handed blow to the side of his face.

He howled and cursed her. She cursed him louder, and the battle was on.

In the next five minutes, Sir Jonas and the Gypsy learned that the heavyset woman was the man's wife, that she had learned that he had not one but two mistresses, and that she had finally caught him on his way to meet one of them.

The argument raged on for a full ten minutes, with the wife buffeting the husband until he finally fled the compartment and the car, with her at his heels.

Sir Jonas looked at the Gypsy and they both burst out laughing.

"A man must check his behind before he looks to service his front," the Gypsy cackled, extending a flask. "A drink, monsieur? It is the finest cognac."

With tears of laughter in his eyes, Avery accepted the flask.

He saw the first blow coming as he upended the flask, but he couldn't avoid it completely. He rolled to his side, but the chop hit the left side of his neck, driving him to the floor.

He managed to free the automatic from his belt, but a well-aimed kick sent it flying from his hand.

The Gypsy moved with swift, deadly precision. In a split second he was on his feet, looming over the huddled figure of the diplomat. He swung his arm, the hard edge of his left hand chopping with brutal force across Avery's throat. He saw the head loll sideways and down, like that of a rag doll that had lost part of its stuffing.

He studied the man through narrowed eyes for a long moment, considering his next move. Then he took out his handkerchief, bent over, and picked up the gun from the floor. That was the trouble with damned amateurs, he thought impatiently. They never learned until it was too late that a gun was more of a liability than an asset.

Swiftly he went through Avery's pockets. He found little that was revealing. That in itself told him much of what he wanted to know. There were no letters, no cards, nothing but the false passport and an old wallet stuffed with bills. He slipped the bills into his own pocket and returned the wallet to Sir Jonas's jacket.

That done, he stepped to one side and slid open the compartment door. The long corridor was empty. The men's lavatory was just two doors down, at the end of the car. He walked to it and tried the door. It was open and the space was unoccupied. Coming back, he glanced in casually at the two compartments he passed.

One was empty. In the other, a young couple were taking almost full advantage of their supposed privacy. Both of the boy's hands were working feverishly under the girl's blouse while their faces were glued together.

Back in the compartment, the Gypsy bent over Sir Jonas again, feeling his pulse. He wasn't particularly surprised to discover that Avery was dead. The vicious chop against the man's windpipe had been more than strong enough to inflict death.

The Gypsy had meant it to be.

He pulled the lifeless man to his feet, supporting him upright with an arm across his back and a hand held tight under an armpit. He slid the door open again and stuck his head into the corridor.

It was clear.

Half carrying and half dragging his unwieldy burden, the Gypsy made for the *toilette*. Inside, he propped the dead man up on the commode seat.

Then, still using his handkerchief, he took the automatic out of his pocket, adjusted it carefully in Avery's right hand, held it against the right temple, and squeezed the trigger.

The Gypsy jammed the lock on the door after closing it, and returned to his compartment.

The coast road from Finike to Antalya wound down into little sheltered harbors and up again to the heights above

them. It sometimes hugged the rocky hillside to escape the
sea, and sometimes arched over the landward end of the
small peninsulas that jutted out every few miles.

The road was little more than a rocky track that ran
through deserted stone villages that had flourished ages before, when Greek and Roman ships sailed the nearby seas.

Twenty years before, when the Citroën was new, its
hydraulic shock absorber system would have taken even
these goat paths with ease. Now the shock absorber system, like its air conditioner, was shot, and the battered old
machine seemed to drop off the end of the earth in jarring
shocks with every pothole.

All the windows were open, but even the car's speed,
such as it was, didn't cut the air's hellish heat. In the rear,
sweat poured down Assim Kalvar's neck and collected inside his shirt. Occasionally he rubbed his back against the
seat as though he had an itch. The bodyguard who sat beside Kalvar did the same.

The driver, a Turkish army major assigned to Kalvar
during his exile from Cyprus, seemed immune to the bone-
jarring ruts and the heat.

"How much farther?" Kalvar asked wearily.

"About an hour, maybe a little more," the major replied.
"We top this last mountain, it's all downhill. Better road."

"Thank God," Kalvar mumbled, leaning forward to get
a better view around the driver.

The old Citroën bounced and squeaked and groaned.
Ahead, Kalvar saw foothills. If they rose high enough, it
would be cooler. He found himself praying for high peaks
despite the car's obvious frailty in such terrain.

They started climbing. The road seemed to end abruptly
against a sheer wall of rock. He stared at stone, vines, and
stunted trees. Then they climbed another fifty yards and a
curve came into sight.

The road wound around it like a slithering snake. The

major slowed. They kept climbing, although more gradually, and started around the curve.

Then they saw the van.

"Shit," the major hissed, and slowed even more, his right hand leaving the wheel to caress the Ingram machine pistol on the seat beside him.

The bodyguard in the rear pulled a large magnum revolver from a shoulder holster under his jacket.

The hood of the van was up and they could see spumes of gray steam spewing from the engine compartment.

"Keep going," Kalvar growled.

"I can't get around him," the driver replied.

A slender young man in a grimy white shirt and dark trousers appeared around the front of the van. His dark curly hair was plastered to his head with sweat, and he sported a sheepish grin. As he approached the Citroën he held his hands out from his side in a shrugging gesture.

"I am sorry. My engine overheated during the climb."

"Can't you move it to the side?" the major hissed, the machine pistol in his lap, cocked and ready.

"Yes, yes, only a minute or two. I have a jerry can of water in the back."

"Be quick about it," Kalvar barked from the back. "We are in a hurry!"

"Yes, of course," the young man said, his face showing shock and fear when he saw the guns. "I am sorry, only a minute, I promise you."

He practically ran to the rear of the van. As he approached, the doors were suddenly thrown open and he dropped to the ground.

The first burst from the Czech 59 shattered the windshield and tore the Turkish major's head from his body.

By the time the barrel of the gun swung back, the bodyguard was diving over the front seat, his magnum firing blindly.

Kalvar saw the man's body dancing. It was literally driven back into him by the pounding of the 7.62 slugs. Blood and flesh splattered him as he slithered from beneath the body and yanked at the door handle.

By the time he rolled from the car, the firing had stopped. He hit the soft tar on his knees and rolled to his feet.

The big man behind the machine gun was looping a new belt into the breech.

Kalvar ran.

He felt the first slug tear into his side, spinning him around.

A crease, his mind recorded, *not fatal. Run for the rocks*.

Then the second, third, and fourth slugs tore into his chest. The bullets' driving force and his own pain made him reel backward. He felt his feet lifting from the ground, felt himself plunging and jumping. Another burst ripped into his head with a bone-shattering crunch. He fell into the dirt, feeling himself die, tasting blood in his mouth. He grunted. Tried to roll away.

His muscles twitched spasmodically, clinging to life even though he had already been dead for several seconds.

FIVE

It was just after dawn when they dropped down out of the hills toward the seaside town of Ayvalik. For the past hour Carter had fiddled with the car radio trying to find something besides blaring, Middle Eastern music.

And then he did, an early-morning newscast.

Carter's Turkish was barely conversational. Reela interpreted as the newscaster shotgunned his words.

"The police found the bodies . . . five dead . . . one critically wounded . . . he's in a comatose state and not expected to survive . . . none identified as yet but one of the dead is believed to be an American . . . oh, my God . . ."

"What?" Carter hissed.

"Turkish military security has been brought into the case. They received an anonymous tip on the telephone."

"Me?" Carter said, already guessing the answer.

Reela nodded. "The caller identified you by name as being involved. Nick, they have a description and the license plate number of this car. They want you for questioning."

"Great," he growled, "just great. Ten to one it was Vain or one of his people. They would love to have me locked up for a few weeks in a Turkish jail."

"It's going to be tough now," she said. "What do we do?"

"Three things. Find a telephone, get rid of these wheels,

37

and find a place to disappear until we can find a boat. All in that order."

The first proved fairly easy. They were on the outskirts of Ayvalik and businesses were starting to open up for the day. Reela pulled into a gas station. A gnarled old attendant with sleep still in his eyes shuffled out to the car.

Reela kept the old man occupied servicing the car while Carter slipped into the station. The pay telephone on the wall was old and battered but it worked.

After three tries, an operator managed to reach the AXE safe number in London. A sleepy duty officer snapped awake when Carter gave his location and N3 designation.

"The airwaves are humming about you, old man."

"I imagine they are," Carter said. "You know we lost one."

"We assumed that from the commercial broadcasts."

"Any chance I can get a pick-up here?" Carter asked.

"Very unlikely. Your hosts are angry, to say the least. Any chance you can take a Greek island-hopping vacation?"

"If I can last the day I think it can be arranged."

"Afraid you'll have to, old man. Hold for a minute."

It was twenty seconds, and when the voice came back it was considerably calmer.

"Do you know your nearest airport?"

Carter closed his eyes in concentration. The nearest Greek airport would be in Mytilene, on the island of Lesbos. "I do," he said.

"Good. Do you have proper identification?"

"No, and my wife is, of course, traveling with me."

"I see. Then I suggest you have a good lunch before your flight. The Taverna Aegean has excellent moussaka."

"I'll remember that."

"Have a nice flight."

"Thanks," Carter said, and hung up as the old man entered the station, hardly giving Carter a glance.

"Well?" Reela asked, as Carter slid back into the car.

"We're set if we can get to Lesbos. Take the coast road and go south."

The hillsides south of Ayvalik were dotted with houses. They had gone nearly two miles before Carter spotted a likely one.

The house was set well back from the road, partially hidden between two jutting rock cliffs. He had Reela slow down in a pass-by. There were two outbuildings, and the compound itself was covered with a tangle of woods and vines. He could also see fountains in which no water was playing.

"No one home?" Reela asked.

"More likely deserted," Carter replied. "Turn around, go through the gates, and drive right to that building that looks like a stable."

It was indeed a stable, with a rusted chain and padlock securing the door. Carter made short work of the padlock with a tire iron, and Reela drove the car into the corridor between the stalls.

"We abandon it?"

"That's right," Carter said. "C'mon."

"What now?"

"We take off our shoes, tie 'em around our necks, and walk the beach back to Ayvalik, hand in hand like we've been out for a morning stroll."

"And look for a boat?"

"Eventually," he said with a smile. "First we find a taxi driver. That should be easy at the train station."

Her eyes grew wide. "Are you mad?"

"Not really. No matter where you go in the world, my dear, and you need something badly, you can count on a taxi driver to find it. The key is picking the *right* taxi driver. Let's go."

Carter let his glance roll along the line of cabs, the drivers in little groups smoking and swapping lies. Then he saw the one he wanted, a swarthy little man with a constant half-smile under a full mustache and sharp eyes that never stopped moving.

"That one," Carter murmured, nodding toward the man.

Reela moved forward. She exchanged a few words with the man and opened the purse that hung from her shoulder so he could glance down into it. The corners of his mouth lifted and Reela turned back to Carter with a nod.

The two of them climbed into the back as he climbed into the front.

"He knows of a place," she said, "run by his sister."

"What did you tell him?"

"Just what you told me to tell him, that you were running from the police."

"And what did I do?"

"Murder."

Carter shrugged. "Might as well go all the way."

They drove toward the sea, into the clutter of the old city. They settled back and eventually the taxi slowed. They scraped through a narrow cobbled street, turned a corner, and stopped at last in a tiny square, one side of which was a long building of wood that seemed to have emerged at the whim of generations of owners. Parts of it seemed wholly isolated from others. There were three roofs and four entrances, and everywhere tiny, shuttered windows. It was painted a fading green. A tiny sign to the right of the center door welcomed them to the Sultan's Rest.

Carter chuckled.

"What is it?" Reela asked.

"Now I know what happened to the Ottoman Empire."

They followed the driver into a dark, marble-tiled hall-way with a battered desk and a short, stout woman behind it who could only have been the driver's sister. The build was identical and the mustache was close.

The driver exchanged a few quick nods with his sister and then led Carter and Reela up two floors and down a maze of corridors. At a dead end he flung open a door with a flourish.

They stepped into a huge room with an enormous cano-pied bed, more marble flooring, and a vast wooden fan that stirred the sluggish air when the man pressed the switch. Off the bedroom was a bathroom with a copper bath built on the same scale as the bed, and a huge copper shower suspended above it. The man prodded the mattress and grinned, talking very fast.

"What did he say?" Carter whispered.

"That it's a fine bed for making babies," Reela said, and grinned.

"Tell him, swell, and ask him if he knows of anybody with a boat."

She did. "Yes. His brother-in-law is a fisherman."

"Tell him we'd like to do a little fishing tonight, late tonight."

Reela rattled, the driver rattled, and she turned back to Carter. "He says it is possible, but if the fishing is done in Greek waters it can be very expensive."

"How expensive?"

"A thousand . . . American."

"Pay him for the room and tell him to set up the boat for midnight."

She spoke to the little man as she counted out the cash. He bowed to them both and backed out of the room.

"Do you think we can trust him?" Reela asked when he was gone.

Carter nodded. "As long as we're willing to pay more than the police . . . and that's pretty easy in Turkey."

She started to undress. "I'm taking a bath."

"Do that. I'll see if the sister can get us some food."

"Not much for me. I'm too nervous to eat."

He watched her turn away, start for the bathroom, and sensed the sudden tiredness that came over her.

"Reela . . ."

"Yes?" she said without turning.

"I'm going to tell you something you're not going to like."

"Oh?"

"I think Carl covered me and stayed in that house to make up for screwing up."

She whirled. *"What?"*

"He had a tendency to be careless about who he used. I think he used the wrong person or persons for surveillance on that house. I think he knew it. You think about it." He closed the door quietly behind him.

The sister whipped up a huge plate of *dolmades*, vine leaves stuffed with ground meat and rice, found an un-opened bottle of ouzo, and set it all up on a tray with dishes.

When he returned to the room, Reela was standing at the window, pensively smoking. Her hair was damp and she had securely tucked a towel around her in all the right places. Her long, full-thighed legs flowed sensuously below it.

"I've never seen a towel look so good," Carter murmured.

"You're right," she replied, mashing out the cigarette. "He was careless. I often warned him about it."

"Good, then we won't need to talk any more about it," Carter said. "Let's eat."

He opened the ouzo and she put the food on plates and sat down on the bed beside him.

Carter ate as if it were his last meal. Out of the corner of his eye he watched Reela eat slowly, doing a better job on the ouzo than on the food.

When they were finished, she reloaded the tray and set it in the hall. While she checked the underwear she had washed and hung on the shower rack to dry, Carter went through the contents of Lupat Savine's wallet.

"Recognize any of these people?" There were four snapshots. Carter laid them out on the bed.

Reela moved to the side of the bed and glanced at them. "Yes. That's the sister, Deemy."

"Who's the guy cuddling her?"

"I don't know."

"He's in this one with Savine. Recognize any of the other three?"

"No."

The other two shots had been taken in a bar or café. In each of them, Savine had his arms around a pair of girls.

"Recognize any of those ladies?"

"No," Reela replied. "But both of those pictures were taken in a dive called the Caravan Club. I recognize that big painting. It's all the way across the mirror behind the bar."

"That might help," Carter mused.

"What are you thinking?"

"I'm thinking that, even dead, Savine and his sister may still be the only way we can backtrack to Drago Vain."

"Then we're going to Damascus?"

"Maybe," he said, stretching out on the bed. "We'll find out for sure in a couple of days."

Reela slithered across the bed and curled into his arms. He felt her back where the towel had slipped down. For the briefest of seconds he began to get ideas. But sleep claimed him before they did.

Carter's body was suddenly rigid on the bed, his eyes open, his mind alert. Except for the moonlight through the windows and a rectangular shaft of light from the partially opened bathroom door, the room was dark.

What had awakened him?

Reela sensed that he was awake, and sat up beside him. Before she could speak, he put a finger to her lips and pointed at the door.

He knew now. He had heard footsteps on the stairs and then in the hall. But they hadn't continued on past the door to their room.

Now, as they both stared, the doorknob began to turn slowly, first one way and then the other.

"Maybe it's the woman or the taxi driver," Reela whispered.

Carter shook his head, slipped from the bed, and pulled her up beside him. They stood close together, her shoulder touching his arm. He could hear her breathing, shallow and rapid in the deep silence.

There was a metallic scraping against the lock. Carter pulled her toward the center of the room and whispered, "Get into the bathroom."

"What are you going to do?"

"Never mind. Get in there and close the door."

She seemed to understand him. She stared at the turning knob, and then she slipped into the bathroom and closed the door behind her.

Carter moved carefully across the room. He stopped a few feet to the left of the door.

He waited in the darkness, listening to the sound of the tool bite at the lock, trying to breathe deeply and evenly.

He didn't have to wait long. Something snapped in the lock and the door swung inward, letting a bar of light fall from the corridor into the room.

A heavy man's figure came into the room, moving fast in a low, springy crouch. He eased the door shut with a backward swing of his foot, and started for the bed, the faint light glinting on the knife in his hand.

Carter took two steps forward and hurled himself on the man's back, locking his arms to his sides. They went down together, the man grunting and bucking against Carter's weight. There was a bull-like strength in his body. The savage twist of his shoulders almost broke Carter's grip as they hit the floor. They rolled over twice, knocking a lamp against the wall, upsetting a chair. Then the bathroom door opened and light spilled into the room.

Carter saw the knife on the floor, twisted, and kicked it under the bed.

He sensed Reela run behind him, and then saw her tug his Luger from the shoulder rig he had hung on the bed-post.

"No!" he hissed. "No noise!"

With a growl of fury, the man worked his hands up to Carter's locked wrists and pulled them apart. He then rolled away and came bouncing to his feet. He wasted a second peering about for his knife, and then lunged at Carter, his massive hands searching for the Killmaster's throat. There was no expression on his bearded face, but his eyes were intent and full of what seemed to Carter as fear.

He came on again and Carter snapped a hard left into his face. The man shook his head and plowed in, his hands spread, his knees crouched to leap.

Carter knew at that moment he could kill the man easily.

This one was no pro, but to be sure he decided to keep him alive until he could be made to talk.

"Turn on the lights!" Carter hissed.

Reela crossed the room like a deer. She snapped on the switch and the room was flooded with brightness.

Carter shifted sideways, jabbing viciously with both hands. In seconds the man's face had turned to raw meat. Then Carter stepped in, whipping his body around, and went to work on the man's gut.

It didn't take long. Without air and blinded by the swelling of both his eyes, he began to fade. He slipped to his knees and then toppled to his back.

A sound at the door made Carter whirl. It was the taxi driver. He stood, glaring, not at Carter but at the fallen man.

Suddenly he cursed aloud and bolted forward. Carter backed off, ready, but he needn't have bothered. The driver squared away and drop-kicked the man on the floor viciously in the side of his head. He was about to do a follow-up, when Reela's arm yanked him to his toes. At the same time, she drilled the snout of Carter's Luger in his ear and started talking.

They jabbered back and forth for a full minute, so fast that Carter couldn't catch a word. At last there was a break and she translated.

"He says that the shit on the floor is a deckhand on his brother-in-law's boat. He must have overheard them talking and heard about the American with all the money. He swears it is no more than that."

"I think I believe him," Carter growled, catching his breath. "If he were one of Vain's men, he would have come in here with more than just a knife."

"He says the boat is ready," Reela replied. "We can leave at once."

"What about this?" Carter said, motioning to the unconscious man.

Reela asked, got an answer, and interpreted. "He says if you will help carry him, we can go out the back way to his car. He and his brother-in-law will give this one a thief's burial at sea."

SIX

The crossing went without a hitch. The waters between the Turkish coast and the outlying Greek islands were well patrolled, but the cabdriver's brother-in-law knew their schedule better than the contours of his wife's plump body.

Carter and Reela were put ashore in a rocky cove on the island of Lesbos. It was on the island's northern tip, about five miles from the capital of Mytilene.

There were no farewells, only an exchange of money and a nod between the three men. Carter and Reela had barely climbed to a ridge above the rocky shoreline when the boat had already slipped into the mist on its return journey.

"Nick, that man, the deckhand they locked below? Will they really kill and bury him at sea?"

"You should know the answer to that," Carter replied. "You're a Turk. It's a matter of honor. Let's go, this way."

Within minutes gray dawn broke, and it wasn't long before the early-morning Aegean sun began to burn off the fog. They were scarcely through the first of many tiny villages that lined the road to Mytilene when an old man in a cart full of produce overtook them.

Carter waved him down. The Killmaster was on firmer ground here; his Greek was fluent. The farmer was on his way to market in the capital. Carter explained that they had been forced to beach their boat on a sail around the island. Could they get a lift into Mytilene?

For a small fee, yes.

Two hours later, they dropped off the cart and walked until they spotted a small hotel that would more than serve their purpose.

Carter signed the register with a Greek alias to avoid showing a passport, and they were shown to a square, white-walled room on the second floor. Carter tipped the youth and Reela moved to the window. She opened it with a sigh.

"The view is beautiful. It's a pity we're not on holiday."

He followed her gaze along the white, sun-drenched buildings along the marina. The sun was high now, turning the Aegean a deep blue.

"Time enough for a long holiday—if we find Drago Vain before he finds us," Carter said, resting his hands on her full hips.

She turned into him. "Now what?"

"I saw a beauty salon and some boutiques as we came in. Of the two of us, you'll be the easiest to spot if they're looking. Change your appearance as much as possible, and buy some traveling clothes, touristy stuff."

She hurried from the room and Carter stripped. He showered under cold water in an ancient, cracked tub, and shaved carefully in even colder water. Using materials from his kit, he broadened his face with plastic pads in his jowls, and combed gray into his temples. It wasn't a great deal, but hopefully it would alter his look enough.

He was dressing when Reela returned. The transformation was startling.

"Good enough?" she asked, posing before him.

The wig was full, ash blond and nicely coiffed. She had added a large pair of dark sunglasses, and now wore a pair of blue slacks, a loose blouse with puffy short sleeves, and a matching scarf tied loosely around her neck.

Carter smiled. "All you need is makeup to match the wig and a camera around your neck."

"The makeup I bought."

She went to work on her face, and Carter finished dressing. An hour later they were in a taxi heading toward the center of the city.

Carter could see why London had chosen the Taverna Aegean. It was out of the way, the kind of place tourists would only drop into by accident. This would make it easier for them to spot the pilot, and he them.

It was still a bit early for the lunch crowd. Besides the owner behind the bar, the only occupants were three old men playing *xeri* at a rear table.

Carter returned the owner's greeting and ordered ouzo and menus for three. "Our friend will be joining us shortly."

They took a table near the window. The owner's wife hurried the ouzo to them while her husband put a tape in a player behind the bar. In seconds, bouzouki music was telling of death and sacrifice in a mountain battle a hundred years ago.

Reela made a face while Carter ordered sausage and potatoes.

"What is it?" he asked when the woman was out of earshot.

"I hate bouzouki music," she replied.

"Of course you do, you're a Turk. Drink and smile like you enjoy it."

Their man arrived the same time as the food. He looked the part in well-cut fawn trousers with knifelike creases and a matching safari shirt. He was tall and square-jawed, with a lined, tough, tanned face. He paused at the door long enough to adjust his eyes, and spotted them.

A gleaming, toothy smile and five steps brought him to

the table where he lifted and kissed Reela's hand. "Rita, it's lovely to see you again."

She blinked, but before she could speak he turned and grasped Carter's hand. "Howard, how are you?" He slipped into a chair and dropped a thin briefcase on the table as he helped himself to the ouzo.

"How was your flight?" Carter asked.

"From Rome? Splendid. Always love flying at dawn, so peaceful." He drank and lowered his voice. "You're Rita and Howard Hall, Americans. You've been in Greece two weeks, island hopping. The passports are stamped as such. They're in the briefcase. I'll leave it."

"What about photographs?" Carter said.

"We'll do them on the plane. I've filed a flight plan for Athens, so they won't check you here. I'll set down in Athens and you'll have an urgent business call. We'll check out of the country there."

"Where to?" Carter asked.

"Italy, Taranto. And my orders are to get you there post-haste."

"They give you any reasons?"

The pilot shrugged. "None, and I don't ask. What you spooky people do before I pick you up and after I dump you off is none of my business."

The three of them ate in silence. When they were finished, the pilot again kissed Reela's hand and left without a word.

They had coffee to kill another half hour, and cabbed back to the hotel. In the lobby, Carter picked up a newspaper and scanned it as they headed toward their room.

"Did we make page one?" Reela asked.

"No, but look what did."

She glanced at the headline, and at the accompanying story, and gasped.

"Kalvar and Proto in the same day," Carter said dryly. "No wonder they want us posthaste."

The sun was high over the port of Cagliari, and the air was becoming uncomfortably warm and humid. A sultry breeze wafted the stench of the fish market along the street and filled Carlo Zimbatti's nostrils.

Zimbatti had been born in Sardinia and he hated it. He and his three brothers had escaped the island and fled to the north of Italy, Milan, as soon as they were old enough. There, they had prospered.

It had been difficult. The fingers of the Sicilians had been strong, even in Milan. But the Zimbattis, the four sons of Sardinia, had proven to be as ambitious and even more ruthless than their southern neighbors. In time, the four brothers had taken control of the north.

Now, with the offer that had been made to them by the terrorist, Drago Vain, their little empire would be solid.

Carlo Zimbatti turned to the right and entered the piazza, leaving the roar of the docks behind him. He crossed the piazza toward an old mansion with an ornate, wrought-iron balcony and a large courtyard shaded by flowering trees. Two dark-skinned men, their faces scarred by small-pox, looked up as he entered the courtyard.

Zimbatti paused, staring into their hollow, lifeless eyes. He wasn't a timid man. Carlo had made his first bones at the age of eleven in the mountains of Sardinia. By the time he was thirteen and raped his first woman, he had killed three more times. He had lived with others as hard and deadly as himself all his life.

But the men who inhabited the inner circle of Drago Vain could make the sweat pop from his pores.

He nodded and the two men nodded in return. Zimbatti went up the steps and into the house.

It was one of the most expensive of the brothels in Cagliari, with rooms on the upper floors for brief encounters, and suites for those who had money and days to devote to their pleasures. It was run by an old don who often rented his rooms for very discreet meetings.

As he had been instructed, Zimbatti climbed to the second floor. Two more dark-eyed men awaited him. Without a word, he handed over his briefcase and lifted his arms. The briefcase was searched and his body was patted down for a weapon.

One of the men opened the right side of huge double doors, and Zimbatti entered the suite.

A lone man hunkered behind a desk. Nearby, a sofa and a large chair were both adorned with naked women.

Drago Vain uncoiled his six-foot-eight frame from behind the desk and snapped his fingers. The two women wiggled into the adjoining bedroom, closing the door behind them.

Vain moved around the desk, extending his hand. "Carlo, it is good to see you again." His English was thick with his native brogue.

"And you, Drago."

"Sit, sit."

Zimbatti sat, and Vain lumbered back to his chair. For all his size, he moved well. He had a head that didn't match his body, small, with a face like a sparrow. His nose was thin and bony, hanging over a clipped, sharply curved mustache. His lips were thin and seemed always twisted in a perpetual grimace.

"You've heard?"

"Of course," Zimbatti said nodding. "It's in all the papers."

"Then you know I can deliver. With Assim Kalvar and Nikos Proto out of the way, the riots on both sides of the line are already breaking out. Drink?"

A bottle of Irish whiskey appeared on the desk. Zimbatti

shook his head. Vain poured a water glass full and brought it to his lips as he leaned back and put his boots on the desk.

Zimbatti noted that the man's tired brown suit had greasy pocket edges. A handkerchief like a large dirty white flower blossomed from the breast pocket. His shirt was canary yellow and equally as dingy.

The man, Zimbatti thought, *is a slob . . . but as dangerous as he is filthy.*

"The Englishman from the U.N., Sir Jonas Avery. . ."

"What about him?" Vain said, belching and refilling his glass.

"My brothers are a little worried. They think there might be repercussions. It could bring in—"

"It was necessary!" Vain interrupted with a bellow. "The bloody Brit has friends on Cyprus. If I left him alive, people would have listened to him. He might have been able to put another of his bloody peace meetings together!"

Zimbatti shrugged and opened his briefcase. "It's your plan."

Vain's feet hit the floor. "You're bloody right it's my plan, and it'll work." Here Vain's voice got low and he leaned over the desk until Zimbatti winced from his breath. "It's my Cypriots that are in place now . . . my own hand-picked politicians. When I give the word, they'll have the rabble back up in arms and the cry will be Cyprus for the bloody Cypriots!"

Zimbatti lit a small cigar, sat back, and let the Irishman rave. He had heard it all, or most of it, before.

"And then, when the time is right, they'll make peace between themselves. The bloody U.N. will be gone, and the Turks and Greeks will get out because they're tired of the bleeding mess themselves. And when me two proud patriotic Cypriots are runnin' the country, it'll be old Drago what's pullin' the strings."

"Well and good," Zimbatti replied, his voice controlled, modulated. "But taking over an entire country is expensive. It's our money that is financing your takeover."

"It is that, but you'll make a hundred times yer money back when I give you a bloody free port to move yer dope through!"

"True, but my brothers and I would like some insurance that you'll keep your part of the bargain once we have kept ours."

Vain's eyes narrowed. "Ya know there's others itchin' fer what I'm offerin' you?" he snarled.

"Perhaps," Zimbatti replied calmly, smiling. "But the Sicilians don't control the product out of Lebanon and Turkey that we do. They can grow without Cyprus. So you see, Drago, we need each other."

Drago Vain upended his glass of whiskey and, for several seconds, glared at the other man. "All right. What kind of bloody insurance do ya want?"

"These." Zimbatti spread a set of papers on the desk. "I want them signed by you and your two Cypriot politicians. When that's done and back in my hands, your freighter full of arms and the cash to hire your expensive mercenaries will be on the way."

Vain scanned one set of papers and broke out in laughter. "Bloody papers. What do you think this is, some kind of legal corporation? What good are these?"

Zimbatti stood and, grinning, leaned forward with both hands flat on the top of the desk. "If we don't get proper return on our investment, a set of these papers will be sent to the Turkish and Greek governments. Twenty-four hours later, Drago, you'll have troops from both countries breathing down your neck. You can't fight them."

"You dumb Dago bastard," Vain hissed, "you won't do that. You and yer bloody brothers would be cuttin yer own throats!"

"I don't think so. If you notice, your agreement is with a holding company in Geneva. By the time the papers are passed over, the company will be gone and its owners untraceable."

Zimbatti gave the Irishman enough time to boil, and then continued.

"So, if you want to rule your own little country, you bloody Paddy pig, sign. And this time you come to us to deliver them."

For the briefest of seconds, Zimbatti thought the other man would lose it and come over the desk after him.

But that point passed, and with a shaky hand Drago Vain reached for his bottle.

Carlo Zimbatti snapped his briefcase closed, turned, and walked from the room, knowing that he had won.

SEVEN

They had taken off from Athens in a torrential down-pour. The sun was just disappearing over the horizon and it was warm and clear when they landed at Taranto, Italy.

Two customs officials came on board, did a perfunctory examination of the plane and their passports, and departed. They were scarcely gone when a lone driver in a dark Mercedes arrived. He hopped out and came aboard.

"Good evening, Mr. Carter. I'm Nate Chisholm. Welcome to Taranto."

He flipped open his credentials case. Carter gave it a glance while the other man's eyes raked Reela up and down.

"Reela Zahedi, Istanbul," Carter said.

"Be with you in just a minute." He moved forward, exchanged a few words with the pilot, and returned to grab their bags. "The man is here. I had instructions to hold the plane. You might be needing it again . . . soon."

"Terrific," Carter groaned.

The "man" was David Hawk, the acerbic and near genius head of AXE. If Hawk had flown in personally from Washington to debrief them, it meant that big things had happened in the time it had taken to get them out of Turkey.

The Mercedes moved silently through the city to the industrialized suburbs away from the sea.

"There," Chisholm pointed as he eased the car to the curb.

It was an old building with rusted iron gratings over the windows and paint peeling off the stucco.

Chisholm killed the engine and leaned back in the seat, obviously preparing for a long wait. Carter and Reela slipped from the car and crossed the street. At the front door a sleepy-eyed man moved out of the shadows. He eyeballed them both and nodded.

"Second floor."

By the time they were through the door he had slipped back into the shadows.

The stairs were old and a bit creaky but, unlike the exterior of the building, spotlessly clean. A blond giant in a parka awaited them at the second-floor landing. Carter recognized him as Judd Harris, one of a revolving team that traveled with Hawk whenever he left the U.S.

"Nick."

"Harris," Carter said with a nod. "Why all the quiet?"

The man shrugged. "Ours is not to reason why. Second door down."

The room was a combination study and office. It had an atmosphere of genteel poverty, its once sumptuous furniture and furnishings shabby from the inroads of time and abuse. There was a gray mist in the room caused by the ever-present cheap cigar clamped in the corner of David Hawk's mouth.

"Any trouble?" That was Hawk's greeting.

"Not once we got out of Turkey," Carter replied.

"Quite a bloody mess." Hawk turned to Reela. "Miss Zahedi, sorry about Hobbs."

Reela said nothing and slipped into a chair. Carter poured coffee from a sideboard and passed a cup to the woman.

"Lupat Savine was fingered," Carter said. "He was tortured, cut up pretty bad before they killed him. He probably told Vain's people enough. That's why they were waiting for us."

Hawk nodded. "Figured as much. Have you heard the news?"

"You mean Proto and Kalvar? Yeah, saw a paper on Lesbos."

"An engineered hit, both of them. Kalvar got it on the road in Turkey with two of his bodyguards. Proto bought it in his villa in Crete. They even made sure they wouldn't have any trouble by taking out his bodyguard, Canavos, first. Blew him up in a hotel bungalow."

"Vain?" Reela asked.

"Maybe. But our research people think they were hired. They would have had to do a lot of open moving around. Since most of the inner circle around Vain are well known and, in most cases, wanted, we think the shooters were hired."

"By Vain?"

Hawk shifted his cigar. "We weren't sure at first, until we heard about Avery."

"Sir Jonas Avery?"

"Yeah," Hawk muttered. "He bought it on a train to Nice. The killer made a halfhearted attempt to make it look like suicide, a bullet in the brain. But his neck was broken first."

Reela's cup clattered against the saucer as she sat it down. "Is there a connection?"

"There sure as hell is," Hawk replied. "We had to lean on Whitehall to get it, though. Sir Jonas had arranged a sit-down in Nice between Kalvar and Proto. Evidently, a peace had already been worked out. All that was left was the signing."

"What makes Vain so interested in Cyprus?" Carter mused aloud.

"If we know who Vain met in that house, we'd have the answer to that," Hawk replied. "As it is, we start from scratch, square one."

Carter lit a cigarette, sat back, and let the smoke drift from his nostrils. "Drago Vain is hot. We and several other agencies have had the clamps on him for a long time. He and his people can hardly make a move. Less than a handful of countries will let him reside . . . none of those will let him operate from inside."

Hawk removed the cigar and allowed a rare smile to split his seamed face. "In general, that's what the computer boys have come up with. Drago Vain's on the sharp edge. He needs a place to operate out of, where no one can touch him."

"Cyprus," Reela whispered.

"It would fit," Carter said. "He gets rid of Kalvar and Proto—"

"And, naturally, riots erupt all over the island," Hawk finished. "It's already starting."

"He's got Cypriot politicos in his pocket," Carter hissed. "That's what the meeting in Turkey was all about."

Hawk shrugged. "It's the best theory yet. It would take men and money . . . *lots* of men and money. Our people in Marseilles, Paris, and Rome say that the word is out for mercenaries. It's a high-paying, long-term contract, the kind that would lure men no one else would hire."

"The real killers," Carter said.

Hawk broke the cellophane on a new cigar. "The way I see it, we've got two ways to go. Vain has to hide until he can move into Cyprus, until his little revolution gains momentum and his hand-picked politicians can glean favor with the people."

Carter paced. "Find him in his hole and gas him out first. We've been trying to do that for months, without much luck."

"True," Hawk said, "but we have to keep trying. The second, at-hand solution, is to chop off his money supply. If we can make his backers lose interest in Vain's Cyprus scheme, it just might flush him into the open."

Carter and Reela exchanged glances. "The sister," Reela murmured.

Carter removed the contents of Lupat's wallet from his pockets and spread the photographs on the desk. "Reela's contact to Savine was through his sister, Deemy. She—or someone in these pictures—might lead us to one or more of Savine's cronies."

"Slim," Hawk rasped, "damn slim."

"But all we've got," Carter said.

"Where is the sister?"

"Damascus," Reela replied. "Vain's people are probably looking for her, but I might get to her first."

Hawk looked up at Carter from hooded eyes. "Damascus?"

"I know," Carter said, "but there's a guy who can get me in, if I can find him."

Hawk turned back to Reela. "How soon can you leave?"

"Now. I've still got cover through a Turkish newspaper. I can go in from Rome."

Hawk worried his cigar for a full minute before raking them both again with his glare. "It's risky as hell, but it's all we've got. You'll be going in cold. We don't have a soul inside Syria."

Carter smiled. "If I can find the man I want, he's all I'll need."

The jangling telephone brought Deemy Savine upright in bed, her eyes wide, her mind instantly alert.

"Yes?"

"Deemy, it's Adib. We're back."

"Lupat?"

"He's here, with me. There has been an accident. . . ."

"What happened?"

"Nothing serious, Deemy. It was an auto accident just over the frontier. Lupat has been hurt. He wants to see you. I'll pick you up in twenty minutes." The phone went dead.

Deemy Savine replaced the receiver on its cradle and closed her eyes in concentration.

It's a dangerous game, Deemy. Never trust anyone, believe nothing anyone tells you. If the word does not come from me directly, there is no word.

She opened her eyes and the image of Adib Bizri's sweaty, pockmarked face seemed to form on the wall. Bizri, who hated her brother, would be the last to call.

Quickly she picked up the phone and dialed a number from memory. After three rings, a sleepy female voice answered.

"Magine, it's Deemy. Have you heard from Lupat?"

"No. Has he returned?"

"I don't know. Did he make his check-in call last night?"

"No, nor the night before. Deemy, is something wrong?"

"I don't know. Get yourself ready to travel. I may see you very soon."

"Deemy, what's wrong? Did something happen to Lupat . . . ?"

"Just do as I tell you," Deemy replied, cutting off the girl's whining voice.

It didn't work, Deemy thought. Something went wrong. Even if Lupat were alive and injured, Adib would be the last man her brother would send to fetch her.

Adib Bizri, if you ever touch my sister again, even try to touch her, I will slice your belly open and feed you your own entrails.

No, she thought, Lupat would never send Adib—with

his grasping hands and drooling lips—to her in the middle of the night.

Deemy moved quickly. She dressed in a black sweater, dark jeans, and soft-soled shoes. For what she would soon have to do, a skirt would be in the way.

From a closet she took a briefcase and opened it on the bed. The briefcase was layered with bundles of American hundred-dollar bills, one half of the Turkish woman's payment for Lupat's betrayal. On top of the bills were two French passports, one for her and one for Magine, Lupat's whining whore.

More of Lupat's last words came back to her: *I will phone you when it is done. We will meet in Paris.*

In her heart she knew she would never see her brother again. She hated the great whining cow, Magine, but she owed it to her brother to take the woman with her.

The briefcase also contained Lupat's coded address book and an American Smith & Wesson .38 revolver. As Deemy checked the loads in the revolver, she wished it were equipped with a silencer.

But it wasn't, so she would have to make do with something else.

From a drawer she took a necklace of fake gold coins. It was heavy and threaded with triple strands of strong nylon line.

Outside, she heard the soft purr of an automobile engine. She padded to the window as she unclasped the necklace.

It was Adib Bizri and a driver. Bizri got out of the car and paused to glance up at her window. She shrank back out of sight and waited.

Bizri spoke to the driver and started across the street. Deemy sighed with relief when she saw the other man remain behind the wheel.

Quickly, she unlatched the door and turned on the small

light in the bath. She left the bathroom door open a crack and moved to the wall. She wrapped a scarf around her hand, then twisted the end of the necklace over the scarf and swung the whole in an arc around her head.

The weight of the heavy coins made it sing viciously as it spun, and brought a smile to her face.

She relaxed every muscle in her body as Bizri rapped on the door.

"Deemy?"

She turned her face away from the door and cupped a hand over her lips. "The door is open, Adib. I am in the bath."

The door opened and Bizri's thin, wiry body entered the room. He moved toward the bath, his figure outlined perfectly in the shaft of light.

"Deemy...?"

The last sound he heard was the whir of the necklace before it curled around his neck.

The coins slapped into Deemy's free hand. Her knee slammed into his back and she hauled hard on the chain, twisting at the same time to take up the slack.

The man's yell was muted to a surprised, gurgling gasp. Her arms strained as she forced his head back. There was a sharp crack, and Adib Bizri was dead.

Deemy loosened her hold and the body slipped to the floor. She turned him over and grimaced when she saw his face. Then she thought of her brother, and her face turned to stone as she searched him.

In his right trouser pocket she found the knife he always carried, the knife he had once floated in front of her face with one hand as he used the other to maul her breasts.

It was an enormous clasp knife with a single blade. She touched a button at its base and the blade flicked out, leaf-pointed, one edge ground razor sharp. She tested the balance and found it perfect.

In one move she grabbed the briefcase and moved into the hall. She walked calmly down the two flights and boldly through the door into the street.

The driver was dozing. He came up out of the seat when Deemy's body cut off the light from a nearby streetlamp.

He looked alarmed.

Deemy smiled and he rolled the window down, his face forced into a grin.

"Adib is making a call. He'll be right down. Shall I sit in the rear?"

The driver looked puzzled, but stretched his left arm over the seat to open the door for her.

Deemy had been holding the knife just behind her thigh. Now she brought it up in a swift movement. The driver was stretched out in an awkward position.

He never saw, and barely felt, the blade plunge into his neck.

EIGHT

Carter sat in his room in the Rome Hilton, thoroughly exhausted. In the last thirty-six hours, he had been to Tel Aviv, Tunis, Casablanca, and back to Rome. The constant traveling had worn him down, especially when he had discovered that the man he sought was already in Rome and had been for over a year.

Reela would have been in Damascus for nearly a day now. Hopefully she would have located Lupat Savine's sister, Deemy.

He munched a sandwich, drank a beer, and waited for the call from Chartim El-Rashad, known in his own circles as the Prince.

The phone rang and he grabbed it. "Hello?"

"Carter, you've been making a lot of phone calls."

"And doing a lot of traveling."

A chuckle from the other end of the line. "I heard. I haven't been in Tunis for two years. What's up?"

"I want to meet."

"That's difficult. If I am seen with you I might get a bad name."

"You mean your old name," Carter said.

"Exactly. I am Louis Corot now, a Beirut refugee dealing in antiquities."

"You mean stolen antiquities," Carter chuckled.

"Is there any difference?"

"It's a one-time job," Carter said, "in and out. Pays well."

"Then it's worth talking about, isn't it. The entrance to the Palatine Gardens off the Via di San Gregorio. One hour."

The line went dead and Carter shrugged into the shoulder rig and a lightweight jacket. He checked the clip in the Luger and hit the elevator.

He had done a lot of running in the last day and a half to a lot of cities. He still wasn't sure how many informants Drago Vain had, but he wasn't taking any chances that he had been spotted. He needed The Prince, and he didn't want to bring anything down on the man.

He spent nearly the entire hour taking taxis crisscrossing Rome. When he wasn't in a cab he was ducking through department stores and passing through cafés from the front and out the rear entrances into alleys and away to another cab.

Exactly one hour after leaving his hotel, he stepped from the last cab at the Forum and walked the few blocks to the Palatine Gardens entrance.

He had stopped only long enough to light a cigarette when a dark green Porsche nosed down in front of him and the passenger door flew open.

"Get in!"

Carter's butt barely hit the expensive leather when the powerful little car's acceleration threw him back with a couple of G forces.

"Getting a little chunky around the middle, aren't you?"

Carter managed to exhale and roll his eyes to the driver. The Prince was a man of medium height, chunky and muscular. His face—even sporting a few days of dark bristly beard—was cinema handsome. The eyes returning his look were as cold and deadly as Carter remembered.

"Age," Carter responded, "gets to us all."

"Not me. I'm gonna stay young forever and then die."

They drove down from the hill toward the Tiber into one of the older sections of the city. Eventually the Porsche slid into an alley that hadn't seen the sun for a couple of centuries and halted in front of a worn, two-story house.

"This belongs to a friend. I use it now and then when he is away on business. This way."

He led Carter inside and up a set of shaky stairs. They moved down a hallway and through a door. It was a small room with a sofa, a vanity and stool, and an unmade bed. A woman with a pouty mouth sat at the vanity brushing her hair.

"I told you to go," the Prince growled.

She rolled her eyes up coyly and made her pouty mouth smile. She was a big girl, voluptuous in a tight red dress. Her hair was as black as her eyes and very glossy. "I know," she said. "You told me."

The Prince looked at Carter and sighed. "I try to be a gentleman," he said. "It was always my wish as a boy. To be a gentleman."

Abruptly, his hand flashed out, and he smacked the girl across the butt. She gasped, more from the suddenness of the move than the pain.

His face blank, the Prince held the door wide and nodded toward her. She was struggling to control her features and maintain her dignity. She stood, threw her shoulders back, and walked out. He shut the door softly behind her.

"I have only wine," he said, going to the desk and removing a bottle. "Will that do?"

"Yes," Carter said.

"You are agreeable today, my friend," the Prince said, pouring two glasses. "Do you need me very badly?"

"Of course not."

The other man laughed aloud. "Then I will only charge

my regular fee, as long as there is no killing. I have given up killing."

Carter shrugged. "I can't guarantee."

"Twenty thousand, five thousand bonus for everybody, plus expenses."

"You don't know the job yet," Carter said.

The Prince waved his glass. "What matters the job? You pay me, I do it."

"What's your nationality these days?"

"Italian. I have been Italian for nearly a year, since my Moroccan passport expired."

"Do you still have your connections in Beirut and Damascus?"

"A few."

"I need to get into Damascus," Carter said, "and I can't go legal. They would like to talk to me about a little affair a few months back."

"What else?"

"Cover my ass while I'm there and bring us back out."

"Us?" The Prince said, his eyebrows going up. "How many us?"

"Two, maybe three," Carter replied. "The other two will be women. Are you interested?"

"Of course I am interested. My current business is very slow. When do you want to go?"

"Yesterday."

The Prince sighed. "Ah, you Americans. You fuck something up today and you want it fixed yesterday. Return to your hotel. I will call you, hopefully by tonight."

Carter moved to the door, paused, and turned. "I feel I must be honest with you."

The cold, hard eyes stared at him. "How nice of you."

"It's a termination. The eventual target is Drago Vain."

The Prince downed the rest of his wine. "I will pretend I didn't hear you. Even a great man such as myself, a descendant of desert kings, only has so much courage."

Carter walked several blocks, constantly checking over his shoulder before taking a cab back to the hotel.

Dusk had brought rain to Rome. Carter could hear the drops beating against the hotel room window. Distant thunder rumbled, and there was an occasional flicker of lightning.

He had called AXE in Washington. Surveillance was tough in Cyprus, but London had helped out and managed to put some men on Vain's suspected politicos, Todales and Zeneer. So far, there was little doubt that the two men were fomenting a resurrection in their respective camps.

There was no word on Drago Vain's whereabouts, nor had international monetary research come up with any shift of funds that would point to the Irish terrorist.

Carter still had the gut feeling that the center of Vain's operation was somewhere in Syria or Lebanon. He could only hope that the contacts he would make in Damascus would lead him to the man before that base was moved to Cyprus.

He started to shake a cigarette out of his pack, then stopped and put it back. His mouth was raw and his tongue numb from smoking.

He was reaching for the phone when it rang.

"Yes?"

"We're in luck. Some people remembered old favors. Get to a lobby phone and call me back at 61-4551."

Carter put on his jacket and took the elevator to the lobby. The other phone picked up on the first ring.

"What have you got?"

"There is a ten-twenty El Al flight to Tel Aviv tonight. Will you have visa problems?"

"Not if I can use my own passport," Carter replied.

"No problem. There is a Karbat tour leaving for the

Galilee from the King George tomorrow morning at nine. The tour spends the night in Safed. In the artists' quarter there is a restaurant called Trafail. Have a late dinner. Your companion will join you. Got it so far?"

"Got it," Carter said.

"Leave everything, like arms and identification, in a locker in Tel Aviv. Tonight you will dine at Alfredo's. It's only three blocks from your hotel."

"I know it," Carter said.

"Good. A Lebanese passport and means of identifying yourself in Safed will be given to you by a man named Georgio."

"How will he know me?"

The Prince chuckled. "I have described to him your honest face in detail. I'll see you in Lebanon."

"Prince, you're a magician."

"I am that, and a greedy one. Give the first payment of my fee to Georgio. Besides being an excellent thief, he is my part-time banker."

Carter killed the connection and dialed El Al Airlines. He made a reservation on the ten-twenty flight to Tel Aviv, hung up, and walked to the front desk. There he requested his bill and rather loudly had the switchboard operator make him a reservation on that evening's Air France flight to Paris.

Back in his room, he packed and placed Wilhelmina, his 9mm Luger, and his stiletto in a custom-made, locked case.

At the front desk he paid his bill and added a fee for placing the case in the hotel safe until he returned to Rome in a week's time.

On the street, he ignored the line of waiting taxis in front of the hotel and walked a few blocks until he saw a cruising cab. Inside, he made a mental note of the driver's name and number, and leaned over the seat.

"Name your fee to the airport and I will double it for a favor. Understand?"

"Signore, for a double fee I will fly you to the airport."

The man named a figure. Carter jotted his name on the back of a hotel envelope, put the money in American currency inside it, and passed it to the driver.

"I want you to check my bag in a locker, put the key in this envelope, and leave it at the El Al counter."

"No problem, signore."

Carter patted him on the shoulder. "I'm sure it will be done, Luigi Belli, Number 724311B."

The look on the driver's face as Carter left the cab told him that indeed it would be done.

On the street, Carter turned the collar of his raincoat up and trotted to Alfredo's.

In the restaurant, he sat at a corner table. It was still early in the evening. The only other people there were tourists, looking forlornly at each other and wondering where the Italians were. Carter knew that no self-respecting Italian would sit down to dinner before nine-thirty.

Perhaps, he thought, that was why they did it . . . to avoid the tourists.

After twenty minutes, a swarthy man carrying a newspaper joined him. He set the newspaper down on Carter's side of the table and signaled the waiter.

"Just wine," he said, and turned to Carter when the man left. "I am Georgio. Louis sends his regards and wishes you a safe journey." He patted the paper.

Carter lifted a corner slightly and saw the passport. "How is it?"

"Not bad," the man said, and shrugged. "Good, actually —the likeness is excellent if you don't shave tomorrow."

"When does it expire?"

"Three years. It's almost new."

"The name?"

"Stassis, born in Beirut, travels to Europe every month."

"Any chance he'll report it stolen before I can use it?"

"Hardly," Georgio smiled. "He likes to indulge when he comes to Rome. Right now he's passed out between two whores in Carbona. He will likely stay that way for a week."

"Sounds fine," Carter said.

The man looked hurt. "I thought it was masterful. You have something for me?"

Carter glanced around the room. "Envelope, my right jacket pocket."

Carter didn't even feel the man's deft fingers relieve him of the money.

Georgio finished his wine with chitchat about the weather, and took his leave after sliding half of a jaggedly torn thousand-lire note under the base of his glass.

Before the waiter arrived again with his food, Carter palmed the half note and replaced it with a whole one from the roll in his pocket. He ate his meal leisurely and caught a cab to the airport, arriving exactly thirty minutes before flight time.

The tour bus was nearly full, some forty people including the driver and a young female guide. Most were Americans, with a sprinkling of French, Japanese, and Dutch.

Carter chose a seat beside a plump matron from Miami. A half hour outside Tel Aviv, heading north, he wished he hadn't.

"My brother-in-law fools around, you know. It's digusting. Sixty years old, the man, with three grown children and five grandchildren. It's disgusting, my poor sister."

Tubas was a rest stop. Carter moved to another seat beside a young rabbi from New York.

"Your first time in Israel?"

"Yes."

"It's a troubled land."

He didn't utter another word the rest of the day.

They did the Sea of Galilee and lunched in Tiberias. In the afternoon they toured along the seacoast, stopping at Migdal, Tabgha, and the Mount of the Beatitudes. It was dusk when they skirted the Jermak range and climbed the steep road to Safed.

As the group checked in to the hotel, Carter made a point of complaining to their guide of stomach pains.

"Then you won't be taking the evening tour of Safed?"

"I think I'll just have a quiet meal and get some sleep."

The girl shrugged and went on shepherding the rest of her flock to their proper rooms. Carter napped until nine, dressed, and hit the street.

He walked Jerusalem Street in the general direction of the artists' quarter, and got directions to the Trafail Restaurant from a cigarette vendor.

The restaurant was crowded with small tables and a long counter along one wall sagging under a variety of appetizers and salads. The aroma of felafel and moussaka floating from the kitchen reminded him how long it had been since lunch.

Carter had just ordered a second aperitif when a young girl of about sixteen appeared at his elbow.

"Sorry I'm late."

She kissed him on both cheeks and slid into the opposite chair. A little above medium height and slender, she was only slightly boyish in an oversize man's shirt and figure-hugging jeans. A curtain of glossy black hair fell from a center part to her shoulders.

As she jabbered inanely about everything from the weather to the events of her day, she slid the torn half of a thousand-lire note across the face of the table.

Carter matched it with his half, and slid the whole note into his pocket.

They ordered and chatted through the meal like old friends. Over coffee, her voice dropped to a whisper and she got to the point.

"You've made arrangements to leave the tour?"

"I've started," Carter replied.

"At midnight, leave your hotel by the rear entrance. I'll be waiting for you in the alley."

Ten minutes later, she stood, kissed him again on both cheeks, and disappeared.

Carter paid the bill and returned to the hotel. He left a note with the tour guide telling her that he had evidently contracted some stomach virus and would not continue with her on to Haifa and Tel Aviv. He paid three days in advance with the concierge, and requested that he not be disturbed.

In the room, he changed into a heavy dark pullover and dark trousers. He put his own passport and wallet in an envelope and addressed it to himself at the King George in Tel Aviv.

At exactly midnight, he slipped down to the lobby. He mailed the envelope and moved down a long, dark corridor to the door of the kitchen. It was unlocked. At the other side of the kitchen was a rear exit.

One step into the alley and she appeared from the shadows.

"You have your Lebanese passport?"

"I do," he said. "Do you have a name?"

"Isella. This way."

She walked quickly, her earthy intensity given expression by a swinging stride. The car, an aging Mercedes, waited at the end of the alley. A dark-skinned man sat behind the wheel, a loose shirt covering his chest, his hair very black and hanging in strips.

She opened the rear door and Carter got in. She had barely settled in beside him when the car lurched forward. In minutes they had left the center of the town heading north.

"We're going over the frontier in a car?" Carter asked.

"No. You'll see."

Carter leaned back and lit a cigarette. The car, its yellow headlights barely piercing the inky darkness, followed the paved road for over an hour. When they veered off onto what was little more than a dirt path, he was sure they were near the frontier.

Abruptly, they rounded a curve and the car rocked to a stop beside a small hut.

"We get out here," Isella announced.

The car door had scarcely closed behind them when the Mercedes made a U-turn and was gone. Carter followed the girl around the hut. A gnarled old man leaned against a horse-drawn cart, smoking. Isella barely glanced at him and they exchanged no conversation.

"We're going across in this?"

Her teeth flashed in a smile. "They search people coming in, rarely going out. But it is safer to be careful."

The rear of the cart was loaded with produce. It was cleverly arranged over a wide strip of canvas. Isella and the old man lifted the canvas. She crawled in and Carter joined her. She exchanged a few words with the old man in Arabic, and darkness swallowed them.

Seconds later, the cart was moving, rumbling and swaying from side to side.

The space was small. Carter felt Isella's body worm its way into his until they were like two spoons in a drawer.

"It will be about three hours," she whispered. "We might as well sleep."

Sleep? Carter thought. *Ridiculous.*

But in minutes the slow swaying of the cart worked its magic and he felt himself drifting off.

It was dawn when the cart stopped. The girl was already awake, shaking Carter gently.

"We're here."

The words were barely out of her mouth when the end of the canvas was raised and the old man was beckoning them out.

Carter slid from the cart. He rubbed the sleep from his eyes and stomped his legs to restore the circulation.

They were somewhere on a mountain. There was nothing to see but other rocky mountains, bare save for a few goats and sheep grazing idly on sparse grass.

"Where the hell are we?" he asked.

"Druse country," Isella replied. "The frontier is back there. Damascus is that way, Beirut there."

As she spoke, a battered Peugeot rumbled up the rocky tract and stopped beside them. The driver was the same greasy-haired man who had picked them up the previous night in the Mercedes.

"He will take you the rest of the way," Isella said.

"What about you?"

"I will go back with my grandfather."

She hopped onto the cart beside the old man. He hissed at the horse and they moved down the rutted lane and out of sight.

Carter moved to the idling Peugeot and climbed into the rear. The car was moving before he was properly settled in the seat.

In no time they dropped out of the hills and gained a paved road. Shortly, the countryside grew greener and undulating. The driver speeded up, but after a few miles slowed.

"Road check," he pointed. Two Jeeps were pulled up on

each side of the road. Three men were by each Jeep. They wore dark green fatigues and red berets. The sun glinted off the machine pistols slung over their shoulders. "You speak Arabic?"

"Well enough," Carter replied.

"Give me your passport. You sleep, I talk."

Carter handed the Lebanese passport over to the man and curled up in the seat. He draped one arm over his face and kept one eye open.

The driver stopped, got out, and met one of the soldiers in front of the car. The passports were checked, and then the shouting started. Both the driver and the soldier stomped their feet, waved their arms, and screamed directly into each other's faces.

Carter wasn't alarmed. He knew that in this part of the world it was the normal way of doing business.

He was alarmed, however, when they moved to the rear of the car and the driver was forced to open the trunk. The soldier found nothing, which incensed him further.

Suddenly the door beside Carter was yanked open. He recognized the Arabic command "Out!"

He crawled out and leaned against the side of the car, forcing his hands to remain steady as he lit a cigarette.

A second soldier came forward and the two of them began taking the interior of the car apart. The seats were thrown out, the glove compartment was searched, and the side panels on the doors were unscrewed enough to probe behind.

A half hour of this and they gave up. They cursed the driver and walked away. The dark little man pulled a screwdriver from his own pocket and, chuckling, went to work on the door panels. Searches of this kind must have been common. In no time the door panels were secure, the seats were back in place, and they were on their way.

"What were they looking for?" Carter asked.

"Dope," the driver replied. "Dumb bastards. I took it through the other way two hours ago, through another checkpoint."

"Weren't you searched there?" Carter asked.

"Of course. And I paid. These idiots couldn't believe I was coming through empty."

They drove for a while longer and the driver pulled off the main road onto a rutted track. He tossed a colored scarf over the seat.

"Put that around your eyes and tie it tight."

Carter did a good job of it, knowing it would be examined.

"Turn your head. Good. Relax, it will be about an hour."

They drove deeper into the country, Carter making no attempt to assess their direction. There was a period when the driver used a confusing series of turnoffs, but the effort was wasted on Carter. He couldn't have cared less where he was going, as long as the man he now knew as Louis Corot was at the end of the trip.

He dozed.

It was about an hour later when the car turned into an even rougher road, slowed, and stopped.

A hand grasped Carter by the elbow and helped him from the car. He was moved about a step. A door was opened and he entered a room to the smell of freshly baked bread.

Fingers fumbled at his blindfold, and then he was staring into the Prince's smiling face.

"Welcome to Damascus."

NINE

The house was only a way station. According to the Prince, it belonged to a friend. He didn't say what kind of friend, and Carter didn't ask.

As soon as it was dark they would be driven into Damascus where an apartment had been set up for their use.

In the meantime, Carter was shown to a bedroom. Fresh clothes were laid out on the bed, all in his sizes. A razor and toothbrush, still in their packages, were laid out in the bathroom. He showered, shaved, and dressed, then rejoined the Prince in the large main room of the house.

Over a couple of drinks, Carter explained the situation in detail.

"And what happens if your lady friend can't find this Deemy?"

"We start hunting ourselves," Carter replied. "Savine's sister is the only line we have, Chartim."

The Prince grimaced. "Do me a favor. Chartim El-Rashad is very dead. Call me Louis."

"Done," Carter said.

The other man poured fresh drinks and reseated himself. "If Drago Vain and his people are here in Damascus, they are probably looking for Deemy Savine as well."

Carter nodded. "But I mean to find her first."

Louis Corot smiled. "Well, it might not be a big problem. I find I still have a lot of old friends here. Let's eat and then we'll check out your lady friend and the Caravan Club."

At dusk they left the "friend's" house in an ancient Fiat. Once again Carter was blindfolded for the first hour of the drive.

"Surely you know by now that I can keep my mouth shut," he growled.

Louis Corot chuckled. "It is for you own safety as well, my friend. What you do not know cannot kill you. It is better that you don't know where you have been."

Outside the walls of the old city, the blindfold was removed. Minutes later they were stopped for a police check. Their passports were perused, then they were passed into the city with a shrug.

The apartment was in the newer section of the city, a gleaming, twenty-story structure. It was less than five years old, but was already showing its age.

Corot shrugged. "When you build from sand, on sand, nothing lasts."

The apartment itself was second-floor rear, its terrace directly over a swimming pool. Carter nodded his approval. If a hasty escape were necessary, they could do it with only a soaking for their trouble. The kitchen and bar were both well stocked, and the telephone worked.

Carter looked up the number of the Orient Palace Hotel and dialed. When the connection was made, he handed the instrument to Corot. In rapid-fire Arabic, the man asked for the flower and gift shop in the lobby. When they came on, he inquired if the flowers he had requested earlier had been sent to Madame Zahedi's suite.

He waited, nodded, and turned to Carter. "They were sent up to her suite within an hour of my call from the villa."

Carter sighed and moved to the bar. "Okay, then she knows we're here."

He checked his watch. Seven. Reela would meet him in the Caravan Club at midnight.

Magine Pelleur looked French. She had a perfect, compact body of flowing, rounded curves from her melon-shaped breasts to her narrow waistline which spread to round, compact hips and exquisite legs.

Her beautiful body was both her fortune and her curse. But Magine didn't really know why. In all of her twenty-seven years she had never harbored an intelligent or logical thought in her lovely head.

Two years earlier, she had been a dancer in one of the more sleazy bars in Pigalle. Even now, Magine could only remember the dancing part. She forgot the last part of the act where she and another girl did a bed show in front of a few dozen slobbering men.

And then she had met the sheik. At least he *said* he was a sheik. He talked her into coming to Damascus. He would lavish her with gifts, set her up in an apartment. She would be his hostess, his right hand, his lover, perhaps one day a part of his harem.

The "sheik" turned out to be a carpet trader, and Magine had "intimately entertained" at least fifteen of his best customers before she got the real drift.

The carpet trader disappeared and Magine went to work dancing again at the Caravan Club. It wasn't too much different from the club in Pigalle. She wore a belly dancer's costume in the main front room. In smaller, private rooms, she danced naked.

But she didn't have to roll around on beds with other girls.

Then she met Lupat Savine. It was love at first sight. He was darkly handsome, and dangerous. He was going to take her back to Paris and marry her. All he had to do was one piece of work and they and his sister would run.

He moved her to another apartment and told her to wait for him. He cautioned her not to tell any of her old friends at the club where she was.

But Lupat hadn't come back. Deemy had come. Just the two of them were going to Paris. She would say nothing about Lupat.

It was all very confusing.

There was a light rap on the door. Magine grabbed a thin robe from a hook on the bathroom wall and padded across the room. She was reaching for the chain, when she remembered Deemy's last words: *Don't answer the phone and don't answer the door. Don't let anyone but me in. Understand?*

"Who is it?"

"Magine, it's me, Lupat. Open the door."

The voice was muffled, barely distinct. But the voice claimed to be Lupat's. That was all that mattered to Magine.

She unchained the door, flipped the lock, and opened it with a welcoming smile.

It wasn't one man, it was two, and neither of them was Lupat Savine.

Their eyes were like black ice as they pushed her backward and slammed the door. One was tall and slim, with a ragged scar across his right ear that had healed over with a lot of bunched tissue. The other man looked like a professional fighter, with scar tissue around his eyes and a flattened nose.

They moved as one through the door, pushing Magine before them back into the room. The tall one closed the door while the squat one pushed his face close to hers.

"Where is she?"

"Huh . . . who?"

"Deemy Savine." His eyes tore at the cleavage that

showed at the neck of her robe, and at the way the cloth kept falling apart to expose her thighs.

She belted the robe tighter. "I don't know a Deemy Savine. I am French, I—"

Her words were cut short when he suddenly grabbed at the robe and tore it part of the way from Magine's body in one violent, ripping motion. At the same time, his other hand struck her a stinging blow across the face.

Magine yelped and fell backward. She was nude to the waist, the robe clinging only to the swell of her hips. She was breathing hard, a red welt on her cheek where the man's fingers had raked her.

"We know you are Savine's whore. His sister would have contacted you. Where is she?"

The taller one had moved into the bedroom. Now he emerged. "She was packing."

The squat one smiled. "Where? Where were you going tonight of all nights?"

"To Paris."

"Where were you to meet Deemy Savine?"

"I wasn't."

He struck her again. She stumbled back several steps, trying to pull the robe back up over her body. She was unsuccessful. Both men's eyes raked her body and then exchanged glances.

Her hip struck the edge of the sofa and she fell to the floor. At the same time, her heel caught on the hem of the robe, dragging it clear of her body as she tumbled to the floor. She lay there gasping, trying vainly to hide a part of her nakedness.

"Please . . . please," she whimpered.

The short man bent over her, his ugly face very close to hers. A hand ran over one smooth hip. "She called you, didn't she?"

"Yes."

"What did she say?"

"That she was leaving the country."

"How?"

Magine's mind rarely worked very fast. Now it seemed slower than a snail as it tried to put words in her mouth. "Fly. She was flying out tonight."

"And you?" the tall one said.

"I was to meet her."

"Where?"

"In Paris."

"When were you flying out?" the short one demanded.

"Tomorrow. I was leaving tomorrow."

"What time?"

"I don't know," she wailed.

The man's face darkened. He pulled her savagely to her feet. The robe remained on the floor. "You're lying, whore. She is as smart as you are stupid. She knows the police are watching the airport. She killed two of our people. . . ."

Magine's eyes rolled back in her head and a tiny wail slipped from her lips. "She didn't tell me she had killed anyone. . . ."

Then they were both on her, the tall one curling his fingers in her hair, yanking her head back. "Then she was here?"

"Yes . . . yes."

"What did she tell you to do?" the short one hissed, his spittle spraying her face.

"Wait for her. She knows a man who can smuggle us to the coast, through Lebanon."

"And then?"

"She was going to arrange for a boat."

"How long has she been gone?"

Suddenly Magine realized what she was doing. Her jaw clamped shut and her eyes blazed at them.

The short one saw it and hit her in the stomach with his balled fist. She cried out and tumbled to the floor again, dazed. He kicked her in the side and then the tall one hauled her back to her feet.

"How long!" he growled, crouching over her.

"Almost two hours. She told me to be packed and ready to leave when she returned."

The two men exchanged smiles.

"We'll wait," the tall one said, letting his hands run roughly over the woman's breasts and stomach and thighs.

The short one began unfastening his trousers.

The Caravan Club was on a tiny street less than two hundred yards long and barely wide enough for the passage of an automobile. By day it was a strip of dingy little shops and cafés from which came the smells of cooking and dust and produce. By night the shops were shuttered and the only light came from the garish fronts of bars and night-clubs.

In the cobweb of streets surrounding the area, one could gamble, be beaten up or knifed, buy drugs, have the pick of women of every hue or simpering boys, and, if one were so inclined, honestly believe you were having a good time "seeing life."

Corot parked several blocks from the street. Outside, he melted into the shadows and Carter took the direct route, right through the whores, the panhandlers, and the leather jackets that eyed everything from his haircut to his boots.

One of them got brave and stepped in front of him. "A cigarette, monsieur?" he said in French.

"I don't smoke," Carter said, slowing his pace but still moving.

"Then, monsieur, enough piasters to buy a smoke?"

Carter stopped. "Very well."

Slowly he took his hand from his pocket. In it was a

Syrian one-pound note. He held it out to the boy, who smiled.

As he reached for it, Carter grabbed the wrist of his right hand. He caught the right elbow with his left hand and yanked forward. The top of the Killmaster's head collided with the center of the boy's face with a sickening crunch.

There was no sound as the would-be thief crumpled to the pavement, his nose pouring blood, his bottom teeth protruding through his lower lip.

Carter looked around.

The boy's leather-clad friends were moving away. The others on the street were looking at the sky as if nothing had happened.

Carter lit a cigarette and walked down the stairs into the Caravan Club.

Inside the entrance was an open horseshoe. The first floor was an enclosed space with a small combo in front of a postage-stamp-sized dance floor. Around the dance floor and around a second-floor balcony there were tables. Most of them were occupied by men wearing themselves out trying to create the illusion of having a good time. The scattering of women among them were interchangeable with the girls on the street outside. Half of them sported youth and luxuriant if impossible bosoms. The other half looked tired and the crow's feet around their eyes were all their own.

Carter spotted a table in a dark corner and headed for it. He was scarcely seated when a waitress, exploding from the top of her dress, appeared. Carter ordered arak and it appeared instantly.

He lit a fresh cigarette off the old butt and checked the room. His eyes passed over Reela twice before he recognized her. She was standing at the end of the bar in quiet conversation with another woman.

She was wearing a sleazy black dress that left no room

for anything underneath it. Only her face and the vee of her breasts above the deep décolletage were discernible. Her makeup was layered on.

Carter smiled at her over his glass. She smiled back and said something to the other woman, who looked Carter's way. This went on for ten minutes, then Reela swiveled to his table.

"Is monsieur lonely?"

"Monsieur is always lonely."

She had barely slid into the other chair when the waitress appeared with what Carter supposed was sold as a champagne cocktail. The waitress scooped all of Carter's change from the table to her tray and left.

He leaned forward, lit the cigarette Reela had produced from a tiny black clutch purse. "Interesting disguise."

"Can you think of a better way to move around this street?"

"No," he replied. "Did you actually get a job?"

"No. The girls from the street can cruise in here as long as they get the suckers to buy these." She lifted the drink and made a face.

"Where are we?" Carter said, barely moving his lips.

"In the dark, I'm afraid. Deemy Savine has flown. The police are turning over the city to find her."

"Why?"

"They want to talk to her about two very dead men. One was in her apartment, strangled. The other was in a car on the street outside her apartment, stabbed in the throat."

Carter whistled low. "Sounds like Lupat's little sister can take care of herself. Vain's people?"

She shrugged. "No way to tell, but I would say yes."

Carter sipped the arak, frowning. "Might be a good sign. Could be she's got something they want."

"I'd say everything points that way. I've tried all my contacts and no one knows which way she ran."

"You think she's still in Damascus?"

"I'd say yes. They seem to be still looking for her."

"But we've got nothing."

Reela smiled. "I didn't say that. See the woman I was talking to at the bar?"

Carter rolled his eyes around, took a hard look, and then got it. "She's one of the two in the photograph with Lupat."

"Right. The other woman in the picture is Magine Pelleur. It seems that Lupat fell, very hard."

"And?" Carter said.

"He promised her the world and took her out of here. Evidently, he set her up somewhere in a flat until they could ride off into the sunset together."

Carter smiled over his glass. "You've seen too many American westerns. Where's the flat?"

"That's the problem," Reela sighed, mashing out her cigarette. "She says she doesn't know."

"What's her name?"

"Greta. She's German."

"What did you tell her?" Carter asked.

"That I'm an old friend of Lupat's. He owes me money. I need it."

"And me?"

"You're my pimp."

"Thanks a lot," Carter said, and headed for the bar.

Greta was a sturdy woman with a big-boned look. Her cheeks were a rusty patina, and her hair was dark brown with a touch of gray. Her shoes were run-down, her pantyhose sagged, and her skirt was shiny. A bright red loose-fitting blouse covered an ample bosom. The impression was of a beautiful woman gone to seed.

Except for the eyes. They darted like a ferret's every time a man at the bar brought out his wallet to pay for a drink.

Carter spoke in German. "Greta, my woman tells me you might be able to help us find Lupat Savine."

A shrug. "Haven't seen Lupat in a month."

"And his girlfriend, Magine?"

Another shrug.

Carter laid an American hundred on the bar.

Greta eyed it and her front teeth bit into her bottom lip. "Lupat must owe you a great deal of money."

"A very great deal. I understand his woman, Magine, might know where he is."

The woman licked her lower lip and then bit it again. "She might. She might not."

"And you might know where we can find Magine," Carter growled.

"I told her I didn't know anything."

The Killmaster matched the hundred and slid both bills to a spot in front of her on the bar. Her hands shook as her eyes darted from the bills to Carter's face.

"I don't know the address. I was there only once. I know the building and the flat."

"Then you could take us there."

"Perhaps . . . for another of those."

Carter put a third bill down. Her hand struck like a snake going after a mouse. The Killmaster's hand was quicker. He snatched the bills, tore them in half, and held up one set.

"The other half when I see Magine."

TEN

They used a cab. Greta gave directions to the driver from where she sat in the back seat between Carter and Reela. Every few blocks Carter glanced over his shoulder. He couldn't spot any lights staying with them, but he knew that Louis Corot was there, somewhere.

"There, that building."

It was a run-down apartment building of six or seven stories. Most of the windows facing the front were dark.

Carter directed the driver on past the building two blocks and then around a corner where he parked.

"Which flat?"

"Two D, in the rear," Greta replied, sweat popping out on her upper lip and forehead.

Carter paid the driver and opened the door. "C'mon."

The woman recoiled. "No, give me my money."

"When I see Magine."

"No, I don't go in there."

Carter and Reela exchanged a look. He leaned close to the woman's face. "Who else is in there besides Magine, Greta? Tell me what you know!"

"I—I don't know anything."

His face hardened. "Who else paid you for this address Greta?"

"No one. Let me go. Keep your money."

Carter snatched the purse from her hands as Reela got a

good handful of the woman's hair and yanked her head back. At the same time, she rolled an ugly-looking knife in front of Greta's eyes. The driver sat, smoking, staring forward.

Carter unclasped the purse and lifted out a thick roll of Syrian pounds wrapped in a rubber band.

"That's my money! Give it to me!" she wailed, only the threat of the knife stopping her from going for Carter's eyes.

"You don't make this much in a month on your back, Greta. Who else did you sell Magine to?"

Her jaw set and her eyes flashed.

"Let me," Reela said in a flat monotone.

Carter nodded and tapped the driver on the shoulder. "Let's you and me take a walk," he said in French.

The driver merely nodded and followed Carter down the street. At the end of the block they moved into a doorway. Carter offered his cigarettes. The man took one and Carter lit it and one for himself.

"The wind is warm off the desert at night," Carter commented.

"It is that," the man replied. "The rains will come in a month."

"The rains are good when they come."

There was a yelp of pain from the direction of the car and a stifled scream. The driver didn't blink. He dragged deeply on his cigarette and kept his eyes on Carter. To him this was probably nothing new. As long as he was paid, he knew nothing, saw nothing, and heard less.

They chitchatted for another five minutes, until one of the car doors opened. Carter led the way back.

Reela was on the sidewalk. Greta was curled into a ball in the rear seat, whimpering. The driver crawled behind the wheel without a word.

"Two men came into the club earlier tonight."

"Looking for Magine?"

Reela nodded. "She knew one of them. His name is Assid. He used to come in once in a while with Savine. They gave her a choice . . . two broken arms, or five hundred pounds for the address."

Carter added his half of the torn hundreds to the others in the purse, and tossed it on the back seat. Then he leaned in toward the driver and dropped some bills on the seat beside the man.

"Take her wherever she wants to go, but take your time doing it."

The driver was stoic and his cab was noisy as he dropped the clutch and rattled off down the street.

"Let's go," Carter growled, and he and Reela moved around the corner, watchful for any sign of movement that would tell them of a watcher outside the building.

They spotted nothing.

Beyond the door, a couple of unshaded low-watt bulbs tried unsuccessfully to make the long, narrow lobby look like something other than the innards of a submerged whale.

They hit the rear steps and went up single file, stepping gingerly on each step to avoid squeaks.

Magine's flat was on their left. Even without putting an ear to the door they could hear voices, male voices, low but growlingly insistent. Then there was the resounding slap of flesh on flesh and a cursing female voice.

Carter used sign language to tell Reela what to do. When she nodded her agreement and understanding, he placed his wrist next to her and held up five fingers twice, pointing at their watches. Again she nodded her understanding, and Carter slipped quietly back down the stairs.

There was a rear exit leading into an alley rank with garbage. He stepped from the doorway and melted into the darkness, looking up. The window on the first floor directly above him was dark. The window above it, in Magine's flat, was dimly illuminated.

The fire escape was a single rusty ladder held with cement nails into the side of the building. It stopped at the level of the top of the first-floor window.

Three jumps and he still couldn't reach the bottom rung. He upended a garbage can and crawled on top of it as quietly as possible.

Seven minutes had elapsed.

He grasped the bottom rung of the ladder and hand-walked up it until he got a purchase with his feet. He stopped beside the second-story window and peered cautiously inside.

It was a small bedroom. A woman, nude, lay sprawled across the bed. The door was open into the living room. Carter could see a woman's lap and legs. Her skirt was hitched up to her hips and her ankles were tied together with a pair of pantyhose. He could see the backs of two men, one tall, rail-thin, the other short and stocky.

From the grunts of pain coming through the window, it wasn't hard to figure out what was going on.

Gently he pressed his fingers to the window at the bottom and lifted slowly. It was unlocked. He pressed again, harder, and it inched upward. Breathing shallowly, refusing to bow to eagerness, he raised the window in tiny, slow movements until it was open wide enough for him to crawl through.

He dropped into the room and duck walked to the bed. It took a full minute to study the bruised and bloody face on the bed before he recognized her as the woman in the photo: Magine Pelleur.

Hopefully, that meant that the woman in the living room was Deemy Savine.

He check Magine's pulse. She was alive.

Pulling the Beretta that Corot had given from his belt, he crawled to the door.

The two men were in shirt sleeves, their coats on the floor. They were taking turns working the woman over. From the look of her bruised face, they had been at it for a while.

Carter was about to check his watch, when he didn't have to. There was a sharp rap on the outer door, and Reela's voice.

"Magine, Magine, are you there?"

The two men straightened up, exchanged glances, and moved as one to the door.

Carter sighed with relief. He could have easily put a bullet in both of them and ended it right there. But without a silencer on the Beretta, he would also play hell getting out of the area before it was swarming with military.

Again Reela's voice from the other side of the door. "Magine, it's me. I have the papers your friend wanted me to bring."

Now the two bad boys were instantly alert. Carter could almost read the look that passed between them. The tall one reached for the lock.

Carter heard the lock click, and moved quickly. He came up behind the two men. The short one sensed it first and whirled on Carter.

"Assid!" he cried.

Carter swung, slamming the gun butt across his temple. The man faded and fell, not out, but unable to do any damage for the time being.

Reela burst through the door in a crouch, her knife floating from hand to hand.

"Watch him!" Carter hissed, nodding to the one on the floor and lifting the Beretta toward the taller man called Assid. "Don't do it!"

The words were scarcely out of his mouth when Assid launched his body in a flat dive.

Acting out of instinct, Carter whirled back. But the man's leaping dive caught him at the knees and he felt himself go down, the Beretta falling from his hand. He hit the floor with Assid still clinging to him, brought his left fist around in a short arc, and felt the man roll away. The Killmaster pushed himself to one knee, saw Assid's body diving for the gun on the floor. Carter twisted, kicked out with his foot, and sent the gun skidding and skittering beneath the couch. He made a dive for Assid, but the man rolled again, avoiding Carter's kick, this time diving for the chair where his jacket still hung.

Carter saw him crash into the chair, bowling it over, roll, and come up with a gleaming blade in his hand.

Carter pushed himself up on the balls of his feet as the man came toward him, moving in a semicircle. The man was dangerous now, very dangerous, the knife wedded to him, a weapon he obviously knew well. Assid feinted to the left, then slashed to the right, and Carter pulled back as the blade nicked his shoulder.

He crouched to counter, then pulled away again, the man already in position. Again the wiry figure feinted to the left, and this time Carter was ready for the counter-slash, ducked low, caught the man's wrist, and twisted.

Assid didn't try to pull away. Instead he came forward, using his shoulder, slamming into Carter, twisting away as he did to break the grip on his wrist. Carter got an arm around the man's neck, letting go instantly as the knife swept upward in a deadly, gut-spewing arc. The man spun around, slashing right and left with short, vicious blows, and Carter found himself dancing backward to avoid being ripped.

Out of the corner of his eye he saw Reela moving along

the wall toward the Beretta. Her movement drew half of Assid's attention.

Carter moved.

The knife slashed the air. Carter took the pass and moved in behind it. He chopped the man's wrist, and the blade fell from fingers opened in pain.

Carter followed instantly with a short blow to the face. He struck again, straightening Assid's body against the wall.

Assid twisted, and tried to sink his teeth into Carter's arm. Carter jammed an elbow into the man's throat, pushed, and kept pushing.

It took only a few seconds. There was a gagging sound, the face changed color, and it was over.

Carter let the body slip to the floor, and turned. The short one was crawling to his feet. Carter tensed, but there was no need.

Reela had recovered the Beretta. The man was lurching forward when she brought the barrel down in a crunching blow across the back of his head. Carter tried to stop a second blow as he went down, but she was too quick. There was a dull thud as the man hit the floor, and then silence.

Carter checked. The tall one was alive, but he would be out for hours. Assid was in the same shape.

"Check the hall and stairs. Anyone curious about the noise, tell 'em you and Magine were having a friendly argument."

"Right."

"No problems, show yourself out front. Louis will bring the car up. Tell him to come up here."

Reela was like vapor before a strong wind going out the door. Carter turned to Deemy Savine.

Her eyes were nearly swollen shut, but through the slits he could tell that she was conscious. Her lips worked behind the gag. He pulled it off and went to work on the panty hose that bound her wrists and ankles.

"Who are you?" she mumbled.

"The American."

"How do I know that?"

"Did you recognize Reela?" he barked.

"Yes."

"Then you'll have to take it for granted," he grunted.

He pulled her to her feet. Her legs were rubber and she sagged against him.

"What did they want?"

"Lupat's book," she moaned.

"Do you have it?"

"Yes."

"Is it here?" Carter asked. She was fading. He shook her hard. "Lupat's book, is it here?"

"No . . . my briefcase . . . car trunk . . ."

She passed out.

"Shit," Carter hissed.

Louis Corot bolted into the room and took in the two men on the floor. "They dead?"

"No, but we can't wait around for them to wake up. Take this one down to the car. I'll be right there."

Corot hoisted the woman to his shoulder and went through the door.

Carter padded to the bedroom. Two bags were upended on the floor, clothes strewn everywhere. He chose a light sweater and a pair of slacks. Magine groaned only once as he struggled her battered body into the clothing.

He ran down the stairs with the woman over his shoulder.

On the first floor a door popped open and a horse-faced woman in a ragged housecoat stepped into the hall. She took one look at Carter, Magine's bouncing rear end, and dived back into her flat.

Reela was behind the wheel, the motor running.

Carter stuffed Magine into the rear seat with Corot and Deemy, and dived into the front.

"Drive!"

Reela spun the wheel and tromped the gas. The little car leaped ahead.

"Which way?"

From the rear, Corot barked directions.

"We should have killed those two," Reela said, tires screaming around a corner.

"Don't think so," Carter replied. "She's got something Vain wants . . . Lupat's book, whatever that is. He'll know we've got it now. Let's hope that makes him nice and nervous. Louis?"

"Yeah?"

"You know a doctor who can be trusted?"

"Sure. But there's one problem."

"What's that?"

"He's a vet."

"That's no problem," Carter growled. "Bones is bones and meat is meat."

ELEVEN

"Gin!" Corot exclaimed, laying out his hand with a smile.

"You must cheat," Carter chuckled, leaning back in his chair with a yawn.

"You own me seven hundred and twenty dollars."

"Put it on my tab."

"No way," Corot replied, shuffling the cards. "You get killed tomorrow, I'm out my money."

The door to the bedroom opened and a tall, gaunt man emerged. He had a long, hawklike nose, bushy brows, and walked with his shoulders rounded and his long arms flapping. It gave him the appearance of a bird about to pounce on some prey.

He mumbled something to Corot in Arabic, and got a nod for an answer.

"What did he say?" Carter asked.

"Wants to know if he can have a cup of coffee."

"Jesus," Carter groaned. "What about them? And tell him to speak French."

The man chuckled and poured himself coffee. "I can speak English if you prefer." His accent was pure Oxford.

"Terrific," Carter said, filling his own cup. "How are they?"

"You must understand. I am a veterinarian."

"It's all anatomy," Carter said with a shrug. "What's the score?"

The man was unflappable. He sipped his coffee, set the cup down, and took his time lighting a cigarette.

"Besides facial contusions, the dark-haired woman has two broken ribs and a fractured arm."

"Can she talk?"

"I've given her a sedative."

"Shit," Carter hissed, and added brandy to his coffee.

"The blonde," the man continued, "she should have X-rays."

Carter and Corot exchanged looks.

"Why?" Corot asked.

"Concussion, a bad one. I also think she was raped."

Reela had just emerged from the bedroom. Carter spotted the look of disgust on her face. Her eyes repeated the statement she had made in the car: *We should have killed them*.

"Can they be moved?" Carter asked.

The doctor shrugged. "The brunette . . . yes, after a day or so of rest. The blonde . . . very iffy. It could be dangerous."

"We'll take care of it," Carter said, and nodded to Corot.

He stood and escorted the doctor to the door, slipping a wad of bills into his hand. Carter moved into the bedroom.

Both women looked like hell, but better than they had an hour earlier. They seemed to be resting easily.

He returned to the living room.

"Play some more gin?" Corot asked.

Carter shook his head. "Sleep. We're all going to need it."

The three of them arranged themselves on couches and chairs around the room. Carter was asleep in seconds.

It seemed like the blink of an eye when Reela gently

shook his shoulder. Through the crack in the drapes he could see that the sun was high. His watch said half past noon.

"Deemy is awake. I took some tea in to her."

Carter nodded. "The other one?"

"Still out."

He splashed cold water on his face until everything came into focus. Then he poured a cup of strong coffee and walked into the bedroom.

Deemy Savine's bruised and puffed lips were set in a hard line. Through the swollen slits of her eyes she studied Carter as he took a chair beside the bed.

She was sitting up, sipping the tea. The sheet had slipped to her waist, revealing her breasts. She didn't bother to pull it up.

"How do you feel?"

"How do you think I feel?" she murmured. Her bloodshot, watery eyes looked at him steadily. "Is my brother dead?"

"Yes."

She sighed deeply. "Figures. I told him he had only a twenty-percent chance of pulling it off. What happened?"

Carter told her, most of it. He mentioned the torture, but left out the grisly details of the body when they found it.

None of it seemed to bother her. She just nodded through it, and when she spoke again her voice was a calm monotone.

"So in the end he belched his guts out to save his ass, ratted on you and your people . . . and me as well. The bastard."

Cold, Carter thought, *the lady is very cold*.

"It looks that way," he replied, keeping his own voice under control. "You mentioned a book last night before you passed out."

"Did I?"

He sighed. He dropped his cigarette in the coffee dregs and set it aside. "You mentioned a briefcase in the trunk of a car. You said Lupat's book was in the briefcase. Is that what they were after? The book?"

Deemy got rid of her own cup and crossed her arms under her breasts.

No speak.

"What's in the book?"

Silence.

Carter pulled his chair closer. "What's with you? We saved your ass last night."

"So what."

"To use an old cliché, Deemy, this is bigger than both of us. If there's something in that book that will lead me to Drago Vain or tell me his plans, I want it. Let me tell you something else. Those two last night? You piss me off, lady, and I'm a lot like them."

"How much?" she hissed.

"What?"

"How much is it worth to you?"

"Reela already paid you."

"Half. She paid me half."

Another big sigh. "All right, the other half."

Suddenly the swollen lips managed a smile. "That's good to know. I'll get a bid from them and get back to you." She threw off the covers and started to swing her legs from the bed.

Carter stayed cool. "Where do you think you're going?"

"Paris. We'll negotiate more there."

"What about your friend?" He nodded toward the other bed.

"What about her?"

"She has a concussion. She was raped."

"That's the breaks." Deemy glanced at Magine and shrugged. "I'm taking a bath."

Carter caught her arm and yanked back so hard she almost somersaulted across the sheets. She came out of it with a vicious kick aimed at his groin. He dodged it and slapped her, a full-armed blow. Her head seemed to swivel and she sprawled half on the bed and half off, finally bouncing onto the floor.

"You don't listen so well, do you, lady?"

He was there at once, seizing her by the hair and dragging her across the room. She came screaming and cursing, stumbling and falling after him, trying to sink her fingernails into him as he kept her at arm's length. Whirling suddenly, he put his head down, came up under her flailing arms, scooped her up, and stepped into the bathroom.

He dumped her into the tub and turned the shower on full blast. The cold water hit her and she started to scream in earnest. He brought his hand up hard, open, into her stomach and the scream ended in a gasp as she doubled over.

"Where's the car?"

"Go to hell."

Pressing one hand onto the back of her neck, he forced her to her knees in the tub. Her body shivered, the nipples of her breasts standing out boldly.

He stopped the tub with his free hand and increased the water pressure. It started to rise over her knees and her hips.

"What the hell are you doing?" she cried.

"I'm going to drown you."

"You're crazy, insane!"

"Yep."

He pushed her head under the water, counted to twenty, and pulled her up, sputtering.

"Well?" he hissed.

The reply was mumbled, but he didn't think it was what he wanted.

She went under again.

After the third baptism, she came up with an, "All right, all right!"

Finally, shaking her again, he shut off the water and yanked her naked, wet body from the tub, pushing her into the other room. She tried to turn around and he sent her spinning onto the bed again, and now he saw fear mingling with the defiance in her eyes.

"I'd start talking," he said quietly. "Now that we both know I'm not kidding." He stood before her as she huddled naked on the bed, glowering up at him. "The car."

"It's an old Morris, dark green."

"Yours?"

"No. It belongs to the butcher near my apartment. He's almost blind, can't drive, so I take him anywhere he has to go. In return I use the car whenever I want."

"Where is it?"

She gave him the address of an apartment building near Saladin's Tomb. "It's in the basement garage. The keys are in a magnetic thing under the right front fender."

Carter turned. Reela was in the doorway, glowering. "Was that necessary?"

"Yes. Watch her like a hawk."

He walked into the living room. Corot was up and dressed. "Let's take a ride."

It was all in code. At first they thought it was just an address book. But as they broke more and more of it, they realized that there were dates to go with most of the names, and offhand notations with the dates.

Corot put it together first. "The dates are meetings that took place, and what was discussed."

By late afternoon they had separated what they felt was relevant and irrelevant. Obviously, several of the names were just what they seemed, old girlfriends, acquaintances, even Savine's tailor and a bookmaker in Marseilles.

Deemy sullenly agreed with their presumptions about these names, and they went back to work on the others. Several of them referred to various terrorist activities that Vain's people had taken part in. It was literally a diary of their activities.

After another hour, they narrowed what was left down to ten names. Three of them were in Damascus.

Corot got on the phone to his contacts. It took another hour to put addresses to the three and pin down what they did for an illegal living.

"Pierre Marchand is a mercenary recruiter. He works out of Damascus, Paris, and Rome. Anis Fani is in the government, Ministry of Defense. Javadi Boudia is a deal maker, mostly arms, big stuff. If you want to buy it, he can supply and deliver."

Carter hit the bedroom again. Deemy Savine knew nothing about Marchand or Boudia. She did know about Anis Fani. It was through her and her husband that Vain and his people were allowed to stay in Syria. Twice, Deemy had been the go-between who carried the bribe money to make this possible.

Back in the living room, Carter mulled over the three names. Anis Fani was out. She could offer little in the way of information, and by being in the government it might be dangerous to intimidate her without killing her.

"Marchand and Boudia?" Corot asked.

Carter nodded. "They've both met with Vain or one of his people a dozen times in the last four months. It looks like they are supplying what Vain needs. Make some more calls, Louis. See if your people can get a line on them."

Corot hit the telephone. The feelers went out, and two

hours later they knew where the two men were and would be for most of the evening.

"Reela, get yourself and Deemy ready to move. If we hit tonight with these two, we leave the country."

"What about Magine?"

"Hospital," Carter replied. "We'll drop her on the way out."

TWELVE

Louis Corot knew Damascus well. They drove almost all the way across the city without once using a main thoroughfare. The car was clean and their papers were good, but on the main streets there was always the chance they would be stopped on a whim and questions asked.

As he drove, Corot passed on to Carter the info he had gotten on Marchand and Boudia from his Damascus contacts.

"We'll hit Marchand first," Carter said, passing his Beretta across the seat. "I'll go up, you cover my back."

Minutes later they were in one of the oldest and poorest sections of the sprawling city. Overhead lights gave way to dim streetlights set far apart. The gutters were clotted with garbage and refuse of every description. Faded, dimly lit signs announced small cafés and run-down hotels.

Corot had scarcely parked when ragged teenagers appeared out of the shadows. He passed out warnings along with coins: if the car was not whole when they returned, he would personally molest every boy in the neighborhood.

They walked down the sidewalk to a narrow, four-story building, identical with a dozen others in the block. There was a short stoop of stone stairs, hollowed by use. The door was ajar.

Inside, there were a dozen men lounging at tables drinking glasses of tea or arak. In the rear was a counter

113

and stairs to the next floor. All conversation ceased as they made their way to the counter and the huge black standing behind it.

"Arak," Corot said, and Carter nodded.

Two glasses of the thick, dark liquid were set in front of them, and Carter slid a twenty-pound note toward the black.

"Keep it," he said in French. "Pierre Marchand?"

"Who would like to know?"

"Two gentlemen from Tunis," Corot said, "interested in employment."

A telephone came from beneath the counter. The black spoke quietly into it, and looked up. "Do you have references?"

"Chavis, Tangier," Carter said, "Borosco in Rome. There are others." Both of the men he mentioned were notorious recruiters in their respective areas. Any idiot who would put his ass on the line for a few dollars and a holiday in the jungle had come across one if not both.

"One of you at a time. Second door on the right, upstairs."

Carter moved around the counter and the black stopped him at the foot of the stairs. The frisk was quick and efficient. When the black nodded, Carter headed up the stairs.

Behind him, he heard conversation return to the room. Out of the corner of his eye he saw Louis Corot move around to the end of the counter. From there he could see every man in the room and the big black man's hands.

Carter went up two flights of wooden stairs. The air was close and smelled of heavily spiced, overcooked foods.

He knocked, and the door was opened by a slim, dark-haired girl. She wore a stained red robe that gaped open above the belt, revealing tiny, just-budding breasts. Her skin was flawlessly smooth, the color of creamed coffee, and her eyes were dark and flashing.

From inside, a guttural growl in French. "Bring him in here, girl."

The girl studied Carter, her lips twisting into a leering smile. "Go in," she said, and moved aside a few inches.

Carter moved down a hall and into a living rom of tattered furniture and heavy red drapes. Old newspapers and debris literally covered the floor.

A three-hundred-pound hulk sat at a sturdy wooden table, gorging himself. The table was laden with plates of greasy lamb, chicken, bowls of rice, and various meats wrapped in vine leaves.

"Pierre Marchand?"

The man nodded, belched, and waved Carter to a chair opposite his at the table. The Killmaster leaned forward before he sat. The hulk had a huge napkin draped across his lap. There was another just to the right of his plate, spread. It seemed to cover yet another dish of food.

"What name do you use?"

"Stassis," Carter said, moving the passport just fast enough across the other man's eyes, "for now."

A belch. "One name is as good as another." He picked something from a front tooth. "My supper. You hungry?"

Carter shook his head.

"Arak?"

Carter nodded.

"Girl."

The young girl stepped forward and poured from an earthenware jug. A smile twisted her full red lips as she handed the glass to Carter.

"Enough," Marchand growled. "Go find something to do—play with the television set."

She shrugged and sauntered from the room. Marchand stared after her, smiling at her small round hips and the backs of her brown legs.

"Nice, huh?"

"A little young," Carter replied.

"No. She's thirteen, just right. Bought her from a trader in Azziz over in Jordan." He picked up a peach from the bowl of fruit on the table and bit into it strongly, tearing a chunk free with big white teeth. "How you hear about my contract?"

Carter jiggled a hand from side to side. "On the streets. A man named Savine, Lupat Savine." He watched the slitted eyes in the folds of fat. No reaction.

"Don't know the name, but that means nothing." The peach gone, Marchand dived back into the lamb and rice. "Where you work? Who for?"

Carter rattled off places and names, and added bits and pieces of expertise such as explosives and some high-tech munitions.

"Impressive, very impressive," Marchand said, chewing away vigorously. "Almost too impressive. How come I never meet you before?"

"I never had to work this cheap before," Carter said coolly.

The room reverberated with Marchand's laughter. "I like you." Suddenly the laughter stopped. "But I don't like the shit in your mouth. You're right, though, old Pierre, the fat man, he gets the shit contracts. You don't look like the type takes a shit contract."

"It never hurts to ask," Carter said, tensing his body. "Where's the action and what's the pay?"

The man lowered his fork and looked up at Carter, still smiling slightly. But his slitted brown eyes were irritable. "I can't use you. Now, you be a good boy and take a walk."

Carter persisted. "If it's Drago Vain and Cyprus, I'm interested."

The dark eyes flashed. "I don't know who you are, smartass, but walk now before your lip gets you—"

Carter mashed the table into Marchand's belly before he got all the words out. He went over backward with a roar, and the room shook when he hit the floor. Carter yanked the napkin aside and snapped up the big Webley revolver it had hidden.

Another roar brought Marchand to his feet. He heaved his enormous bulk at Carter, who danced agilely to the side. As the hulk came past, Carter smashed him across the face with the barrel of the Webley. The impact of the blow sent Marchand across the table. Food scattered in every direction, and the big body landed on the floor in the middle of it.

Carter put his knee in the man's gut and squeezed his throat with his left hand. When the mouth opened, he put three inches of the Webley's barrel in Marchand's mouth and rattled it around.

"Listen and listen good, you fat tub of guts. I don't care any more about you than camel shit. I know you're recruiting for Drago Vain."

Blood spewed from the crease in Marchand's cheek, mixing with the lamb grease and gravy. He was breathing rapidly, his eyes flaming in his fat face.

Slowly, Carter removed most of the barrel from his mouth.

Instantly, in a high, screeching voice, he began to curse Carter, spitting out epithets in French and Arabic as if they were dirt he was trying to get off his tongue.

"That's all," Carter said softly. "Don't say anything else."

The Killmaster thumbed back the hammer on the Webley and shoved the barrel as far as he could in the rolls of fat around the man's middle.

"You're just a name on a list. You don't talk, someone will. Good-bye, asshole."

"No, no!" Marchand shrieked. "What do you want to know?"

"Who set up the contract?"

"Vain, it was Drago himself. I met him twice."

"How many men?"

"Fifty, all grunts. I get two hundred English pounds per man."

"Where do they do the time?"

"Cyprus. I deliver them in Tunis, equipped. They ship out on a freighter."

"When?" Carter hissed.

Marchand seemed to have second thoughts. His eyes began darting around the room, and Carter could feel a sudden tenseness in his bulky body. He buried the Webley in fat clear to his wrist.

"Do you know how long it takes to die with a bullet in the gut, Pierre?" he growled. "Now answer my question ... *When?*"

"Two weeks from tomorrow, the seventeenth."

"Good, very good, Marchand. One more to go. Who's the paymaster?"

"I don't know." He howled in pain as Carter put all his weight on the knee in his gut. "I swear I don't know! It comes out of an account in Switzerland, the Credit Suisse Nationale."

Carter stood and headed for the hall.

"Hey, you . . ."

Carter turned. Marchand was on his feet, holding one hand against the angry gash in his cheek. "Yeah?"

"You'll never get out of Damascus alive. I'll come after you."

Carter walked back across the room, hefting the big Webley in his hand. "No, you won't, Pierre." His voice was soft, his smile thin-lipped. "Because if you do, I'll finish this. I'll feed five inches of this in your face and then blow the back of your head off. So you're not coming after me, Pierre. You're going to crawl into a hole until I've got Drago Vain. Because if you don't make contact now and tell him you're off the contract, he'll kill you faster than I will."

Carter turned and slammed from the room, moving quickly down the hall. The child-woman was leaning against the wall by the door. Just as Carter opened it, she came up on her toes and kissed his cheek.

He went quickly down the stairs, the Webley at his side. Corot was at the counter, a Beretta held loosely in each hand. The big black man now sat at one of the tables.

A dozen pair of eyes turned as Carter hit the bottom step. A dozen pair of eyes followed the two of them as they walked back to back to the front door.

On the sidewalk outside, Carter tossed the Webley into an alley.

"Anything?" Corot asked, as the car lurched forward.

"Enough to know we're on the right track. Next stop, Javadi Boudia."

THIRTEEN

Louis Corot moved steadily down the lane. He had both hands tucked into his pockets and he walked with his head down, uninterested in his surroundings. But every detail was being recorded in his memory with the accuracy of a movie camera.

There was plenty of available concealment—high banks, higher than a man in places, topped by hedges which, in the main, were thick and concealing. Confident that he was completely hidden, Corot stopped at a gap and gazed in at the house. Fifty yards of garden, exposed for most of the way unless they could use the cover of a bisecting hedge. Door locked thick and heavy.

He darted into the off-lane and made a complete sweep around the house. By the time he hit the road again, he had seen everything he needed to see. He broke into a jog, and minutes later slid into the car beside Carter.

"Access?" Carter said.

"The doors are out. They are as thick as you are, and bolted from the inside. The second-floor windows look like the best bet. You can go up one of the pillars."

Carter thought for a moment. Corot's contacts had given them a brief sketch of Javadi Boudia's business, and his personality. It was a cash business. Want to start a little war? A big war? Boudia would supply the hardware, the end-user certificates, and the means of transportation. It was strictly a cash transaction, and usually the cash was up-front.

Personally, Boudia was strictly a businessman. He didn't care from whom he bought, nor to whom he sold.

A man like that, Carter thought, would probably listen to reason.

"You take the one in the front," Carter said. "I'll handle the two in the rear and go in. Let's go!"

They split, two shadows merging with the darkness.

The terrain was just as Corot had described it. Carter moved along the perimeter and then glided over a low wall soundlessly to land on the balls of his feet. He moved along the hedges, peering ahead, halting as he saw the dark shape of the man leaning against a tree.

The man was only half alert, and Carter crept cautiously forward, silent and swift. The other man would be in the bushes at the far end of the path. Carter closed in, his blow designed for effectiveness, not sportsmanship, a smashing, straight-armed thrust into the man's throat. He caught the man before he fell, and lowered him silently to the ground.

He moved forward instantly, through the trees. He picked out the second man, squatting down by the house. Carter moved to the edge of the trees, then raced into the open and across the path. The squatting man half turned, saw the figure rushing toward him, started to rise.

He only half made it as Carter bowled into him, carrying him to the ground. Carter delivered a crushing blow into the man's jaw, then got to his feet, lifted the man, and smashed another blow to his jaw. He opened his hand and the figure toppled backward to lie still. He would lie still a long time.

Carter crouched, his ears attuned to any foreign sound in the night. He gave Corot another two minutes to knock out the guard in the front of the house, and then swung up onto the stone veranda.

The pillars were thin, more decorative than support. He used his arms and his knees tightly wrapped around one of the pillars, and seconds later rolled onto the roof.

All the windows on the second floor were dark. He tried each of them on the side that faced him, and found them all locked. For entry, he chose a round, porthole window that dropped into a bath.

He worked quickly, outlining a rectangle in gaffer's tape more than large enough for his body, with the bottom side leading into the caulking at the arched base of the window.

This done, he applied a suction cup to the center of the rectangle, and went to work with a one-inch glass cutter. Finished with that, it took only four light taps with the butt of the Beretta and the pane popped out.

Carefully, he set the glass on the roof and dropped into the bathroom.

The only sound other than his own breathing was music wafting through the house from somewhere below... strings, soft, muted.

Carter checked each of the rooms on the second floor before descending the stairs. Javadi Boudia lived well. The furnishings in each of the bedrooms and a small den were worth a year of Carter's salary.

The only servant was an old lady who slept in a small room in the rear of the house. Carter didn't bother with her. If everything went as he hoped it would, her slumber wouldn't be disturbed.

He gravitated toward the music. It came from behind two large, tile-decorated doors. One of the doors was slightly ajar, just enough so that the Killmaster could survey the room.

It was a spacious office, paneled in rich mahogany. At one end was a sofa and coffee table, then a worktable and several conference chairs. Across the plush rust-colored carpet, at the other end of the room, was a handsome executive-style desk. One entire wall of the office was dominated by large windows that looked out onto the garden courtyard.

The room's only occupant stood by the desk, speaking into a telephone. He was tall and rangy and angular and stoop-shouldered, but he looked very formidable. His face was craggy, deeply lined, with cold black eyes that obviously meant business. A shock of gray hair fell across his forehead. He wore a white silk shirt with a loose tie, and his well-cut suit jacket was on the back of the desk chair.

Carter waited until the, conversation ended and the phone was replaced before he stepped into the room. He stopped just inside the door, the Beretta held loosely in his right hand.

"I want conversation. I don't want to use this, but I will."

No change of expression other than perhaps the essence of a tiny smile. "My son-in-law and his friends?"

"Sleeping peacefully," Carter said. "They'll have headaches tomorrow, little more."

There was no expression on the face or in the black eyes that followed Carter as he closed the door behind him and started forward.

Still unmoving, Boudia sat bent slightly forward at the waist, his left hand resting on the desktop. There was a diamond ring on the little finger of that well-manicured hand, and heavy gold links showed in the French cuff of the silk shirt. But it was the right hand that interested Carter most. The right hand was hidden somewhere below the desk, and it occurred to him now that it might just possibly be holding a gun.

He came slowly forward, his gaze fixed, ready to move faster if he had to. When he reached the desk without starting any reaction, he put both palms on the edge of it and leaned forward. He stayed that way, saying nothing, his gaze intent. It took perhaps three more seconds before any outward sign was reflected on Boudia's hard face.

Something happened then. Carter could not tell what it was, but it seemed to him that the shoulders relaxed beneath the custom-made shirt. An expression that might have been relief flickered in the black eyes. The tight line of the mouth eased somewhat and the thin lips moved.

"I assume this is not a robbery," Boudia said, his English barely accented.

"Not at all."

"Then you can put that away."

Carter slipped the Beretta into his belt and planted one cheek on the desk. "I'm afraid you'll have to do some repair on the round window of the upstairs bath."

Boudia chuckled, almost amused, as if unwanted visitors dropped in on him like this every night. "Whoever you are, I must say you're resourceful. Brandy?"

"Fine," Carter said.

Boudia moved to a sideboard and poured from a crystal decanter. "You've ruled out robbery. If you were here to assassinate me, I would already be dead. What do you want?"

"Information . . . on one of your clients."

"Oh, dear, that's difficult. I have almost a lawyer-client relationship with all of them. Sworn to secrecy, you might say." He handed Carter one of the snifters. "Cheers."

"A long life."

Boudia sipped. "Should I take that as a warning?"

"Let's hope not." Carter drank. It was Napoleon, very good. "You've met three times with Drago Vain in the last four months. What was his order?"

This brought a reaction. The man was good. He tried to hide it, but the question was too abrupt and too much on the mark.

"I see no problem in telling you that, since I declined to do business with the man."

This surprised Carter, but he managed to conceal it. As Boudia reeled off the hardware, grenade launchers, surface-to-surface missiles, and several items of small arms, a pattern emerged.

Carter decided to take a stab in the dark. "And your delivery date was to be sometime in this next week. The place was Tunis. Transportation from there was a freighter."

Another strong reaction and then a noncommittal shrug. "It was," Boudia nodded. "But, as I told you, I didn't take the contract."

Calmly, being careful of his timing, Carter returned his glass to the sideboard. "I think you did."

"No."

"No, you didn't take the contract from Vain. But I think you took it from someone else."

The right hand started to creep back under the desk. Carter's free hand darted forward like a snake and grasped Boudia's wrist. He turned it over and pressed the back of it against the edge of the desk.

"Most unwise, Monsieur Boudia. Until now we have both acted like gentlemen. You'll find it very easy for me to revert to being an animal."

"I do believe you mean it."

"I do, believe me. I won't kill you, but you'll wish I had."

The arm relaxed. Carter released it and opened the drawer. From it he lifted a Ballester Molina .45 automatic.

"Exotic," he murmured, hefting the gun. "From Argentina, isn't it?"

"It is."

Carter freed the magazine and ejected the shell from the chamber. The shell spun across the floor. He pocketed the magazine and dropped the automatic on the desk.

"Now, let me put the picture together as I see it. Drago Vain is a man who usually takes what he wants. That's difficult when it comes to arms. Brokers like yourself aren't exactly a brotherhood, but you do keep each other informed. He strong-arms one of you, no one else would do business with him. Also, the size shipment he needs is expensive. You don't operate on credit, and Vain doesn't have that kind of cash. How am I doing so far?"

Boudia's face was impassive, but his body language told Carter that he was on the right track.

"You agreed to fill the contract only if Vain had a backer, a man—or men—of means that you could trust. Who is it?"

The eyes never wavered. "You put me in a very tight position."

"Not at all," Carter replied. "My source of information is fairly extensive. Eventually I would find out. I just don't want to take the time. You tell me and go on with your business. I'll take it from there."

"You're bucking some pretty heavy people," Boudia declared.

"I'm no virgin at it."

"No," the other man sighed, "I imagine you're not. If I don't deliver, they will simply go to someone else."

"I handle that part of it," Carter said, sure of himself enough now to slip the Beretta back into his belt. "Who is Vain's backer?"

Boudia finished his brandy and tossed the snifter into the fireplace. The sound of the shattering glass reverberated around the room.

"The Zimbatti brothers, in Milan."

"Nice doing business with you, Boudia."

Carter walked to the front door and exited into the night. Louis Corot materialized at once by his side.

"You're smiling."

"Yes, I am," Carter replied. "How long will it take to set us up for an exit out of the country?"

"An hour, no more. Everything's ready and waiting."

Corot drove. They were both silent for the entire trip back to the city. Only when they were climbing to the flat did Corot speak.

"Six hours, we'll be out of Syria."

"That's good," Carter said.

"What happens then?"

"Back to Italy, raise some hell."

"Sounds like fun."

"Your job's done once you get us out of Syria."

"Tell you what," Corot said with a chuckle. I'll stay on for half pay. I hadn't realized how boring my life had become."

Carter glanced over at him. "You're on."

Something was very wrong. They could both sense it the moment they entered the apartment.

"What is it?" Carter asked.

"Magine," Reela whispered. "She never woke up. She's dead."

Carter looked at Corot. "I'll get someone over here to take care of it," Corot growled.

The Killmaster nodded and lit a cigarette as the other man moved to the phone.

FOURTEEN

Carter tossed his bag into the back seat of the taxi and followed it.

"Welcome to Sicily, signore. What hotel?"

"A hotel later, here in Palermo," Carter said. "First I want to go to the Villa Palagonia. Do you know it?"

"*Sì*. It is expensive, twenty kilometers."

"That's all right. I'm a rich American."

The taxi lurched from the curb and Carter leaned back in the seat and rubbed his eyes.

It had been a rough fourteen hours, with little or no sleep. First by truck to the coast and then the transfer to the small fishing boat. Twelve miles out, a chartered seaplane had picked them up and flown them to Tel Aviv. At Lod Airport, a young embassy official ushered them through customs. An hour in the VIP lounge—and a few more strings pulled—put them on the early-morning flight to Rome.

Carter had reclaimed his gear and his own passport from the hotel, and contacted Washington with what he had learned and his plan of attack.

It had taken an hour for the word to come back: *Go for it.*

The second half of Deemy Savine's money was authorized and she was put on a plane for Paris. Reela, Carter, and Louis Corot were glad to be rid of her. She was not the warmest or noblest of people. They all had the mutual feeling that they were transporting a female adder.

Reela and Corot stayed in Rome to await word from Carter, who caught the first available flight to Palermo, Sicily.

"Palagonia, signore. Where do you wish to go?"

"Around the villa, the park by the sea."

The driver made the turn and slowed as he drove through the narrow road through the park.

"Here," Carter said. "Wait." He climbed out of the taxi.

The temperature was a pleasant eighty, but threatening to climb higher as the afternoon wore on. The breeze coming in off the ocean stirred the air, making it comfortably bearable.

Carter checked the park's occupants as he strolled. A man in his sixties sat alone on a bench, reading a paper. Near the playground was a woman in a white starched dress and spotless white shoes. She was busily engaged in rocking a baby carriage and watching over a small boy who was riding around and around in circles on a red tricycle.

Near the rail over the ocean stood a slim, handsome man in his thirties. He was wearing dark sunglasses, a silk shirt opened halfway to his navel, and a pair of expensive tan leather loafers that matched his skintight trousers.

He lit a cigarette and tossed the match toward the ocean as Carter settled against the rail a few feet to his right.

"*Ciao*, Guido," Carter said. "How're you liking it over here?"

"It ain't Manhattan, man."

"It ain't thirty years starin' at bars, either," Carter replied, lighting his own cigarette.

Both men spoke without looking at one another. They smoked, staring straight out to sea. Behind them, the toddler continued his rounds, the circles getting bigger and bigger. The plastic wheels of the tricycle made an annoyingly gritty sound against the bricks and cobbles.

"You got a lot of balls, man, helpin' deport my ass and then callin' me."

"You owe me one, Guido."

A laugh, hoarse, raspy. "Shit."

Carter flipped his cigarette and turned around. He leaned his elbow on the rail and watched the kid on the tricycle.

"I did you a favor that night, Guido."

"Some favor."

"I gave you a choice . . . thirty years, or run. I could have given you another choice. I could have blown you away."

"I gave you the names you wanted."

"True," Carter said. "But the law wouldn't have seen it that way."

"Okay, I owe you one. Whaddaya want?"

"You work for Don Pepe?"

"It ain't exactly a secret."

"I want a meet," Carter said.

Another derisive laugh. "You're outta your mind. The old man don't see nobody, let alone someone with your connections."

"He'll see me, Guido. You tell him who I am, and that I want to talk to him about the Zimbatti brothers in Milan." Out of the corner of his eye, Carter could see the man tense.

"That may not be enough."

"Then you tell him what a bad son of a bitch I am, Guido, and that I know about his son, Giulio."

The silence stretched for several minutes. Finally, Guido turned to face him. "Where you stayin'?"

"Villa Igiea, in Palermo," Carter said, and turned on his heel and walked back to the taxi.

•   •   •

Carter paid the driver and stepped from the cab. There was a busload of tourists arriving at the same time. He let himself get caught up in their flow.

It took a while because of the commotion, but he was finally able to book a room.

The first thing he did was purchase a bathing suit in the hotel sports shop. Then he took the elevator to his room. He was pleased with the accommodations. It was a good-sized room, with a large bathroom and a lovely balcony that overlooked the entire bay. Carter could see the tiny white sails of the boats on the water and hear the delighted cries of the bathers on the beach below.

He changed and went down to the beach. He rented a lounge chair and lay back languidly. In minutes he felt the tension ease from his body and his mind began to work.

Don Pepe Allano, the head of one of the four ruling families in Sicily. Don Pepe was one the first ones in the old days who had expanded to the mainland. Eventually all four families made the move. To avoid war, they had split the territory. Don Pepe had taken northern Italy for his own, with his power base in Milan.

He had ruled it for many years uncontested. Then along came the Zimbatti brothers, four of them, the upstarts from Sardinia. A bloody war broke out, and lasted four years. And then Don Pepe's only son, Giulio, was killed.

It took the heart out of the old man. He pulled in his teeth and gave the Zimbattis Milan. Shortly afterward, he had retired. Don Pepe had very little power now, but he had knowledge. And that was what Carter wanted.

Carter felt his eyes grow heavy. He dozed, and when he awoke, the light had changed. There were fewer people on the beach. He got up, stretched, and walked out into the breakers that were pounding along the shore. He swam out until the hotel looked like a cereal box in the distance.

Then he rolled over on his back and let the tide wash him lazily back to shore.

He took his time ambling back inside and through the lobby. No one even looked at him, let alone made an approach, as he moved to the front desk.

"Carter, six-twenty. Any messages?"

"None, signore."

"Grazie."

He took the elevator up to his room and showered the salt and sand from his body.

At seven, he dressed and went down to the bar. He ordered a local beer and sipped it as he eyed the spectacular sunset dip gold and red over the hills. Sicily was beautiful. What a contrast to its poverty.

He had been in the bar almost an hour when the woman slid onto the stool beside him. She was tanned and seductive in a thin white nylon dress relieved by a leather belt.

"A whiskey, neat," she told the barman, and took a pack of unfiltered cigarettes and a book of paper matches from a small white straw purse. When her drink came and her cigarette was lit, she turned toward Carter. "I'll bet your name is Nick."

"Do you always bet on sure things?" he replied, swiveling the stool to face her.

She leaned her elbows on the bar, narrowing her square shoulders. The tight dress made her seem terribly thin, tiny-breasted and boyish. She wore no jewelry, and her gray cat's eyes were large and luminous. Her cheekbones were high and prominent, the mouth wide, and the light reflected from the window took the color from her cheeks and hollowed them out, giving her a gaunt cast.

"Touché," she murmured, blowing smoke from the side of her mouth. "We have a mutual friend. Guido."

Carter managed not to register any surprise that the contact was a woman, nor show his relief that the contact had been made. "I wouldn't call Guido a friend. Who are you?"

"My name is Simone. Why do you want to see Don Pepe?"

"I told Guido . . ."

"I don't give a shit what you told Guido." Her smile was wide, her teeth starkly white and even. "Tell me."

"Why should I?"

"Because, if you don't, you might as well flap your arms and fly back to where you came from. Don Pepe doesn't get along with the American police."

"I'm not a policeman."

She shrugged, mashed out her cigarette, and slid off the stool. Carter dropped a bill on the bar and followed her into the lobby. He caught her by the elbow as she reached the front entrance.

"I need information, a lot of information."

"What kind of information?"

"About the Zimbatti brothers."

"Look in the files of your FBI," she replied icily.

"I need more than that."

"Why?"

Carter leaned forward until his nostrils filled with her scent. "Because in the next few days I want to become a very large pain in the ass to the Zimbattis."

The big gray eyes narrowed and he could almost see the gears mesh in her brain.

"My car is in the hotel parking lot. This way."

He fell in step beside her. "Don Pepe must trust you a great deal."

"He does. We are very close. Don Pepe is my father."

Now Carter understood the acid in her tone when he'd mentioned the Zimbatti name. Simone Allano, besides being the daughter of Don Pepe, would also be the sister of the butchered son, Giulio.

The car was a fast, low-slung Porsche, and she hit every mountain curve as if she were headed into the stretch of a Grand Prix race.

Carter forgot her driving and concentrated on the beauty of the moonlight glinting off the sea to their left and the mountains to their right.

They flashed through tiny fishing villages, each one like the last. Always there was a square with a three-or-four hundred-year-old church. The stone houses, most of them two or three stories high, were built in tight rows alongside narrow, cobbled streets.

Suddenly she turned off the road onto a small lane. Minutes later, they were running next to a high concrete and stone wall. There was an opening to a driveway, and as Simone turned into it, she blinked the headlights twice.

They glided over a gravel drive, and a figure moved in the shadows at one side. Carter thought he could see the gun cradled in his arms. The walls seemed to be about six feet high, enclosing perhaps an acre of tree-studded lawn and shrubbery. The floodlights had been arranged so that their beams did not light the entire area but only the perimeter of the house, a rambling, one-story structure, its white-painted masonry walls topped by a tile roof.

The car pulled past one wing and stopped in the parking area in front of a three-car garage. Carter followed the woman's lead back around to the front of the house. At the door, a hulking figure in a white shirt and dark beret with a shotgun slung over one shoulder stepped from the shadows.

"You know the procedure," Simone said coolly.

The Killmaster lifted his arms and spread his legs.

When the frisk was done, the big man opened the front door and bowed them into the foyer. It was masonry like the exterior, and directly ahead was a dropped living room.

"This way."

She led him through a living room and along a paneled hall. They passed one closed door, their steps reverberating on the bare wood floor. When they reached a second door, Simone opened it and motioned Carter inside.

"My father is waiting," she said in a low voice.

It was a beam-ceilinged room with paneled walls and bookcases and built-in cabinets. A fireplace yawned in the lower half of one wall, the furniture was heavy-looking, and the rug was thick. The man who rose from the oversize red leather chair under the floor lamp was Don Pepe Allano.

He had the same look Carter remembered from photographs. His tanned face beneath the thinning hair looked smooth and faintly glistening in the lamplight. A large multiple-band radio had been tuned low, and for a moment there was only the shortwave sound of American music in the room.

He cleared his throat and extended his hand. "Good evening, Mr. Carter."

"Don Pepe."

"Have a seat. A drink?"

"Thank you, no."

"Good."

Don Pepe Allano was impressive. He was nearing seventy, but was still handsome and erect. His features seemed benign, but on closer scrutiny Carter saw an immense capacity for cruelty that couldn't be hidden.

It was in the eyes. They were penetratingly sharp and set deeply into a narrow face that appeared long because his hair was straight and combed back from a high forehead. Both cheeks were lightly pocked from a childhood disease; the nose was long and straight, his mouth wide and harsh over a hard, unyielding chin. The overall impression was one of firm, formidable authority.

The eyes scrutinized Carter. There was no humor in them. "What is it you want from me?"

"I assume you have a file on the Zimbattis."

"A file? Why would I have a file on that scum?" Don Pepe snorted.

"I think, Don Pepe, because in your heart you still think vendetta for the way they murdered and butchered your son, Giulio."

Black fire crackled from the old man's eyes for an instant, and then he looked away. "That was years ago. A bitter memory, no more."

"Then I have wasted my time." Carter started to rise, but the man's soft voice brought him back to his chair.

"Why do you want to know about the Zimbattis? Or perhaps I should say, why does the American government come to me to learn about the Zimbattis?"

"They are bankrolling a man we are very interested in."

"So?"

"This man is about to embark on a very large business venture, with the Zimbattis' financial aid. We would like that business venture to fail."

The old man chuckled but there was no humor in the sound. "I will be honest with you, Mr. Carter. There is nothing I would like more in my old age than to see all four of them with coins on their eyes. But I am too old now for war."

"Before it starts, Don Pepe, they will know that it's me on the other side. They will never know the source of the information you give me."

Allano seemed to go inside himself for several moments, digesting both the man, Carter, and his words. When he spoke, it was scarcely above a whisper.

"What do you want to know?"

"Names, first of all. I want the names of every man associated with them. I want the names of their suppliers and their customers. I want addresses and telephone numbers. I want to know who their mistresses are and how often they visit them. I want the make and license plate numbers of their cars. I want—"

Don Pepe held up his hand. "I understand." He stood and his black eyes stared piercingly down at Carter. "Have you had dinner?"

"No."

"This will take some time. I'll have food sent to you."

He left the room, and minutes later his daughter wheeled a tray into the room. It was brimming with aromatic pasta dishes, veal, huge chunks of bread, and wine.

Wordlessly, Simone set a small table between them and served the food.

"*Buon appetito*," she said, and began to eat.

Carter found that he was ravenous. He ate with gusto, almost forgetting that she sat opposite him. He was on his second helping of everything when she spoke at last.

"My father has asked many people about you."

"Oh?"

"You are something of a mystery, an enigma."

"Oh," Carter repeated, not looking at her.

"But with bits and pieces of information, he has put together something of a picture. You are a specialist. You go after hand-picked targets, people who are normally untouchable. It is said that you are the best at quietly doing the job and getting away clean. Is that true?"

Carter slowly sipped his wine and met her stare. "If it is true, if I am that man, then I would be a very foolish man to admit it, wouldn't I?"

Simone took his reply with a nod and went back to her plate. "Will you kill the Zimbattis?"

"Not unless they try to kill me."

"Let's hope they do," she said in a low voice.

An hour later, the old man reentered the room. He handed Carter a manila envelope two inches thick and, without a word, turned and walked back out.

"I'll drive you back to Palermo," the woman said, rising.

In the car, using a small penlight, Carter perused the thick sheaf of neatly typed pages Don Pepe had given him. By the time they pulled into the hotel parking lot, he was satisfied that there wasn't a thing he didn't know about the Zimbattis and their underlings.

"Good night," he said, stepping from the car. "And, thanks."

"Mr. Carter?"

"Yes?"

"Would you like to sleep with me tonight?"

He leaned through the window. "No. You see, I don't like you or your father any more than I like the Zimbattis."

He turned and, whistling softly, walked up the steps and into the hotel.

FIFTEEN

Carter called Reela from the Palermo airport just before his flight.

"I've got everything we'll need. You and Louis get the earliest flight into Genoa."

"Genoa? I thought our targets were in Milan," she replied.

"They are, my love but I don't want any telltale signs of us coming in by air, train, or even a bus. I'm flying to Genoa directly from here. You should arrive before me, so have a car ready."

"Will do. See you soon."

He had a light breakfast and boarded the noon flight. Reela and Corot were waiting for him in the baggage claim area.

"I got a Volvo," Corot said. "It's fairly inconspicuous, but solid and it moves."

"Good."

Twenty minutes later they were on the highway to Milan. Carter drove so that the other two could digest the ream of information he had brought with him from Sicily.

Around five, he stopped in the little village of Lomella for something to eat. He found a little trattoria on the edge of the village that wasn't crowded. He requested a table far in the rear where there were no other customers.

He waited until they were fortified with food and wine before he started.

"Well, what do you think?"

"Fantastic," Corot enthused. "My God, we even know what kind of medicine Carlo Zimbatti uses for his ulcer."

"I can already think of about five stings," Reela added. "Where did you get the information?"

"That's not important," Carter replied. "The man wants nothing to do with this. The important thing is, this stuff is up to date almost to the hour. Louis, you got a safe pad in Milan?"

"No problem. It's a villa on the river about five miles north of the city. Very secluded."

"Who owns it?" Carter asked.

"An old gunrunner. He's doing five years in Ipotsi outside Rome. I negotiated through his daughter. She jumped at the three-grand rent."

"And she'll keep her mouth shut?"

Corot nodded. "She's been in the game damn near as long as I have."

"Good. Let's get moving."

They skirted Milan to the north, and about two miles farther on Carter left the motorway. Another mile and Corot directed Carter off onto a gravel side road.

"Just a little farther," Corot said. "There."

Carter turned into a drive on the left, away from the river. The house wasn't visible from the road because of the thick stand of trees and shrubbery, but there was a chain link fence with a wide gate that stood open. The drive curved slightly and then Carter saw the squarish bungalow with the veranda across the front.

"Looks good," he said. "We can see forever from every side."

The house sat well back from the road. Between it and the river, the villa boasted a semicircular driveway. One big tree shaded the front veranda, and the house was completely surrounded by lawns.

Inside, without speaking, they dumped their bags in the hall and together inspected every room in the villa, each mind committing to memory the layout, the positions of doors and windows, and of every room in relation to the others. They found no one in the house, in the double garage, or on the grounds.

"Louis, you're a genius," Carter said, pulling a bottle from his bag.

"I know."

"Let's have a drink."

They had drinks over a small kitchen table by a window overlooking the river.

"As soon as I stow my gear, I'll fix some dinner," Corot said. "I stashed some groceries in one of my bags."

"I'm afraid you're going to be busy tonight and most of tomorrow," Carter said. "Here's a shopping list."

Louis Corot surveyed the penciled sheet. "No problem on the cars, about an hour. The guns, ditto, maybe a little more time. What do you want with a boat?"

"Insurance," Carter replied. "This place is on the river. If we can't get out of here on the road, we'll go by water."

"Good thinking," Corot said nodding. "The rest of it I can get by tomorrow."

"Make sure of that telephone gear," Carter said. "The one number my man in Sicily couldn't get was Bruno Zimbatti's hot line. I have a feeling that before this is all over we'll need that."

"Right." Corot stowed the contents of his bags and returned with some canned goods and steaks. "Eat well. I'll hike to the village and take a bus into Milan. Don't wait up."

He was out the door, and seconds later the sound of his footsteps faded.

"I'll cook," Reela said.

"You do the cans, I'll do the steaks," Carter offered.

A half hour later they were enjoying the meal. The talk was light, inconsequential, as if neither of them really wanted to discuss why they were there. Then Reela abruptly changed the subject.

"Do you really think this will work, Nick?"

"Yes," he said, "I'm sure of it. Two things that people like the Zimbattis can't take . . . a hard hit in their pocketbooks, and frustration. We'll do both."

"Just the three of us?"

Carter grinned. "Just the three of us. A few days from now, Bruno Zimbatti will back off Drago Vain's deal, and I think he'll hand us Vain on a platter."

"You know what?" she said, shaking her head and grinning back at him. "I believe you."

He pushed away from the table. "Now, me for a shower and shave."

Carter emerged from the bathroom with a towel around his middle. Reela was lying on the bed. Her clothes made a trail from the door to the bed.

Maybe it was just an accident of beautiful physical proportions, or how she lay, or just because it was Reela, but the sight gave Carter's eyes a rare old pleasure.

He sauntered across the room, taking off the towel. As he looked at her, a movement under her closed eyelids told him she was awake. He dropped the towel on a chair and sat on the foot of the bed watching her. There was a glisten of sweat around her lips and on her ribs.

Within a few moments she opened her eyes, turning her head lazily to see him. He shifted up to where he could bend over to put his lips on hers. A smooth arm coiled around his shoulders to keep him close.

"You know," she whispered, "I think Louis's old gunrunner friend is maybe not so old."

"Why?"

"Look."

Carter rolled to his side and looked up. The entire underside of the canopy over the bed was one huge mirror.

"My, my," he chuckled.

"Come here."

She found his lips with hers. They were moist and welcomingly parted. Her tongue glided effortlessly through his lips, prying, opening, until it found his tongue. Quick, darting movements, thrust of a tongue against a tongue, heightened the passion already alive in their bodies.

Then she slowed her tongue and struck up a deliberate tempo, in and out of his mouth. Her legs twisted him over until she was above him.

He kissed her arms and her breasts and her navel. Her hands pushed his head farther down until his tongue found the center of her passion.

"Yes," she hissed, grinding herself against him, "yes, yes, yes."

She began to tremble, and Carter flipped her over onto her back and started all over again. Licking her ears. And her neck. And down along her breasts. And holding them together firmly, his head oscillated as he sucked the nipples. And then down, down he went, licking her stomach, licking her thighs.

Then his head was between her legs and he pulled them up and closed them. His tongue was there, his hot tongue licking, and then his teeth gently nibbling.

She gazed up at the mirror on the ceiling, and could see him, her headless man, his legs outstretched, the muscles of his buttocks taut, his shoulders quivering. Then she could not see him because her eyes were closed and she was rising to him and crying out, her hands pulling at the hair of his head.

He was relentless, his tongue like a whiplash. She tried to push him from her as she squirmed in the shrill ecstasy of climax, but his head remained there like a boulder she couldn't dislodge. Then she shuddered again, her tense body subsiding, and she writhed slowly to his endless oral expertise, watching again in the mirror on the ceiling.

Then he was over her, his hips between her thighs. She arched to meet him and they collided in a bone-jarring thrust.

She made love aggressively, passionately, with complete abandon. A whimper in her throat rose to a moaning scream as they burst together and she felt his hardness going on and on as if forever.

He slid his hands beneath her buttocks and held her, slowing her to his movement until they rode together, each in perfect time with the other. Despite their frenzy and the flow that had already soaked her, it took a long time. They grew comfortable with each other, enjoying the fit. It was she who started the race, nails deep into the thickness of his legs, hauling him into her with each thrust.

"Come on," she gasped. "Come on, come on, come on," bucking each time she made the demand.

Carter tried valiantly to keep up, like a man running for a disappearing train. He just missed. She was already exploding in a back-arching groan when he made it, hurrying the more to finish at the same time. They ended the journey together, limp and exhausted against each other.

"Kiss me," she murmured, and they dozed in each other's arms.

It was about an hour later when Carter was awakened by the low roar of a boat. He padded to the window and parted the drapes.

Louis Corot was just piloting a powerful Corsair inboard

into the little boathouse at the end of the pier.

Carter heard the engine die, and moments later Corot appeared on the pier carrying two bulky cases.

Carter padded back to the bed, smiling.

The Prince, under any name, was one hell of an operator.

SIXTEEN

Carter parked the old Volkswagen 'on Lanzone behind the Basilica di Sant'Ambrogio and walked south through the maze of alleys. When he found Ziatti he turned in and headed for the third building on the right.

Luigi Paladonni was a paid enforcer for the Zimbatti brothers. Two weeks before he had screwed up a job. Now he was on ice until they could smuggle him out of the country. Because of his constant contact with the brothers he was perfect for Carter and company to use for their first move.

Carter mounted the stoop of 114 with the card case palmed in his right hand. Inside the case was the metro detective's badge and the ID Louis Corot has phonied up for the occasion.

He rang the night bell. A stockily built man wearing only a pair of trousers opened the door a few inches and peered out at him with sleep-filled, belligerent eyes.

"What you want?"

Carter held out the badge and let the slanting light from the hallway fall on it. "Talk as natural as you can," he said quietly. "Answer my questions." He raised his voice just enough to carry into the hall behind the man. "Do you have an open room?"

The man cleared his throat and stared at the badge. "We're all full up," he said.

"Think I'd have some better luck somewhere else in the block?"

"Couldn't say for sure. You could try across the street. They might have an extra."

Carter lowered his voice to a whisper. "I want some conversation with the man in number two. You want your permit to operate this fleabag still in force tomorrow morning, you'll go back to bed and forget you ever saw my face."

In Italy you don't mess with the police and you don't mess with the underworld. This man was faced with both and he wanted no part of either.

His eyes became round and solemn. He nodded slowly and jerked his thumb in a furtive gesture to his right. "Just beside me," he said, breathing out the words. "Second room down the hall on the left."

"Thanks, anyway," Carter said loudly, and moved silently past him into the small airless hallway. He closed the front door and pointed to the stairs. The man needed no urging. He took the steps two at a time, his bare feet noiseless on the faded carpet.

Carter waited until he had turned out of sight at the second-floor landing. The he rapped sharply on the door of the second room. His breathing was even and slow, and his hands hung straight down at his sides.

Bedsprings creaked beyond the door and footsteps moved across the floor.

"Who is it?" a voice asked quietly.

"Paladonni?" Carter said in the same low tone.

"Who?"

"I don't got time to piss around, man. I got words for you from Bruno."

"Bruno who?"

"Who the fuck do you think, Bruno. It's time to move. We got a fishing boat in Genoa gonna take you out to a freighter. I'm supposed to drive you."

The door opened an inch and stopped. Carter saw one eye shining softly from the light in the hallway, and below that the cold blue glint of a gun barrel.

"Walk straight in when I open the door," the voice said. "Stop in the middle of the room and don't turn around. Get that straight?"

"Okay, I got it, I got it."

"Start walking."

The door swung open. Carter entered the dark room with the hall light shining on his back. He was a perfect target if the killer wanted to shoot. But he wasn't worried about that. Not yet.

A switch clicked and a bare bulb above his head flooded the room with harsh white light. He heard the door swing shut, a lock click, and then a gun barrel was pressed hard against his spine. The man's free hand went over him with expert speed, found the Beretta, and flipped it free of the holster.

"Lemme look at you now."

Carter turned slowly and backed up slightly so the full glare of the bulb hit his face.

"I never seen you before."

"You ain't supposed to," Carter replied.

Paladonni's youth surprised Carter. He was twenty-four or twenty-five at most, a big muscular kid with tousled blond hair and sullen eyes set close together in a wide brutal face. The gun he held looked like a finger of his huge hand. He was wearing loafers, slacks, and an unbuttoned yellow sport shirt that exposed his solid, hairy chest.

Young, Carter thought, but a different breed than the usual human. He was a hard and savage killer.

"What's so special about you?"

"I'm a cop. If we're stopped on the road between here and Genoa I can get us through."

"A cop?" he said softly, and took a step back from

Carter. He went down in a springy crouch, his sullen eyes narrowing with suspicion. "I don't like. this. The whole deal stinks. I'm the hottest guy in the country right now and they send a cop to bail me out? You got a badge or something?"

"I'll take my case from my jacket pocket," Carter said quietly. "I'll do it nice and slow. You're getting all excited, sonny. What's the matter? This your first job?"

Paladonni swore at him impersonally. Then he said, "I'm making sure it ain't my last, that's all. Take it out."

Carter opened his case and flashed the badge. He held it just far enough from the other man's eyes to make it difficult for sure identification.

Paladonni stared at him, the gun steady in his big fist. "I like this less all the time."

Carter raised his hand casually—as if he were going to scratch his chin—and struck down at the other man's wrist, gambling on Paladonni's momentary confusion and the speed and power of his own body.

He almost lost his bet.

Paladonni jerked back from the blow, his lips flattening in a snarl, and the rock-hard edge of Carter's hand missed his wrist. But it struck the top of his thumb and knocked his finger away from the trigger. For a split second the gun dangled impotently in his hand, and Carter made another desperate bet on himself and whipped a left hook into Paladonni's face.

It would have been safer to try for the gun; if the hook missed, he'd be dead before he could throw another punch. But it didn't miss. Paladonni's head snapped back as Carter's fist exploded under his jaw and the gun spun from his hand to the floor. Carter kicked it under the bed and began to laugh. Then he hit Paladonni in the stomach with a right that raised him two inches off the floor. When the big blond bent over, gasping for breath, Carter brought his knee up into his face and knocked him halfway across the room.

"It was your last job, sonny," he said, grabbing the slack of the sport shirt and pulling him to his feet. "I've got words for Bruno, Pietro, Antonio, and Carlo and you're going to be my messenger boy."

"You're nuts, man. You're outta your goddamned mind. Killin' cops don't mean nothin' to them. . . . "

Carter laughed again and didn't bother to explain. He bent Paladonni's arm up into the center of his back and bounced his head off the wall a couple of times.

"You shut up and listen, listen real good. Someone contacts you every night to make sure you're being a good boy and staying in place. Who is it?"

Nothing.

Carter twisted the arm further until it was right on the edge of breaking. "Who?"

"Bruno . . . Bruno calls me hisself, a booth on the corner. He calls me there every night at eleven."

"Good. I'm putting a list of telelphone numbers in your pocket. Read those numbers off to Bruno and tell him if he's smart, he'll start calling them at midnight tonight."

"That's it?"

"That's it," Carter said, and gave Paladonni a hard right to the kidneys that dropped him to the floor writhing in pain.

Carter retrieved the revolver from under the bed and headed for the street.

Bruno Zimbatti was head of his clan by virtue of age more than anything else. Each of the four brothers was equally ruthless and on a par in cunning, but it was Bruno who was the father figure and made nearly all the final decisions.

He was taller and straighter than a man of his age had a

right to be. He was also less forbidding than a man of his position should have been. His hair was white, but most of it was still covering his head. His eyes were alive, black and piercing. His nose was big but not fleshy. The face was lined, though the flesh was firm and healthy-looking.

"And the nuts are still there," he said aloud, gripping his crotch as he stared at himself in a large mirror.

"Bruno," came his wife's voice from the top of the stairs, "come to bed."

He glanced at his watch. It was eleven sharp.

"I have to make a call," he called back up the stairs, reaching for his private line, the one that had been installed by his own people, the one that the telephone company knew nothing about. "I'll be right up, *cara mia*."

Bruno Zimbatti could hardly know that it would be over fourteen hours until he would be able to put down his head for even a catnap.

Carter was also reading the face of his watch in the light of the streetlamp above the phone booth.

It was 12:15.

Fifteen minutes past the appointed time and the phone had not rung.

But then Carter had not really expected it to ring, not on the first time out. Bruno Zimbatti would scoff at Paladonni's fright. He would wonder how the blond killer had been found and wonder why he was still free, but he would scoff at the idea of anyone giving him an order to call down a list of telephone numbers at an appointed time.

Carter had expected the reaction, planned for it. Now phase two of their little plan would go into operation.

He dropped a coin in the slot and dialed the number of the central police station on the Via Francesco Sforza.

"*Centro*," a bored voice answered.

"I believe the police are looking for a suspect in an

attempted murder, a man named Luigi Paladonni."

"*Sì*," the voice replied, alert and wary now.

"You will find Paladonni at One-fourteen Ziatti. The room is number two."

"And your name, signore?"

Carter paid no attention. "There is a news kiosk at number six Via Falcone. In the rear alley there are two garbage cans. The gun Paladonni used in the murder attempt is in one of those cans."

Carter cut the connection and dropped another coin in the slot. This time he dialed another phone booth in the Piazza Santa Maria Beltrade just a block from the popular nightclub Astoria.

Louis Corot's voice answered on the first ring. "Yes."

"Me. Is little brother Tony still trying to pick up something young and fresh in the Astoria?"

"He is that. Have you had any fresh nothings whispered in your ear?"

"I have not," Carter replied. "Happy fireworks."

"See you on the Monza road," Corot said and hung up.

SEVENTEEN

Antonio Zimbatti was young and handsome with an athlete's six-foot-two body. He had brown curly hair, brown eyes, and by virtue of being a Zimbatti, he was rich.

All of these things made him very attractive to women. He was also the only one of the four Zimbatti brothers who was still single, and Antonio intended to live his life that way.

The girl across from him was eighteen years old and very beautiful. She was five feet tall with high, proud, and round breasts, a snug waist and a lavish behind. All of her attributes were currently being shown off in a simple cotton dress that was cut a bit low and tight in the front.

Tony Zimbatti didn't know her name. He hadn't even asked for it. He had bought her five drinks and for the last hour talked all around the subject that was most on his mind. Now he leaned forward and came directly to the point.

"That dress is very tight."

She giggled. "I know."

"Is there anything under it?"

She giggled some more. "Just me. I never wear underwear. The way I'm built there's no need. I guess I'm lucky."

"I'm the one who's lucky." He eyed the mounds of flesh pushing up so provocatively from the top of the dress and

157

thought up one more question: Didn't that long tendril of hair nestling in the cleft of her bosom tickle?

He decided not to ask it. Instead he asked the big question, the one that had been on his mind since he had seen her walk into the Astoria.

"Why don't we drive over to my place for a quiet drink?"

"Just a drink?" She batted her eyelashes so hard one of them came loose.

"Well, no. I thought that after the drink we could hop into bed."

"Oh, dear, do you think I'm that kind of a girl?"

"Yes, I do. Aren't you?"

The giggle was almost a hiccup. "Yes."

Tony threw some bills on the table and took her arm. He could almost hear the eyeballs move as they followed her movement under the dress.

The maître d' almost tripped opening the door. "Good night, Signor Zimbatti, good night."

Tony passed him a huge bill and guided the girl with his hand on one solid hip. "*Arrivederci, Fonzo, arrivederci.* That's my car just down the street, the white one."

"The Lamborghini?"

"Nothing is too good for my ladies to ride in."

He patted her ass . . .

She giggled . . .

And with a thunderous roar the car disappeared in a bright ball of orange flame.

The blast blew both of them to the pavement. Tony Zimbatti was knocked sprawling and for a tense moment he lay protecting his head with his arms from the shards of flying glass from a nearby window.

The sound wave rolled down the street, faded, and was replaced by another sound, and his stunned ears finally recognized the shouts and cries of many people. One of them was the giggler. She was screaming and running down the street as fast as her tight skirt would let her.

Hands helped him to his feet. "Signor Zimbatti, are you all right?" It was the doorman from the club.

"Yes, yes, but look at my car . . ."

"Signore, I was running after you. There is a call for you in the club."

"A what?"

"Telephone, signore—an emergency."

"Christ."

With one last impassioned look back at what was left of his hundred-and-fifty-million-lire automobile, Tony followed the man back into the club.

"Yes, yes!" he barked into the phone.

"Is this Tony Zimbatti?" The voice was husky and feminine with a strong accent he couldn't spot.

"Yeah, who's this?"

"Too bad, Tony. It was a beautiful car . . ."

He went rigid, his hands shaking. "Who the hell is this?"

"I suggest you call Bruno, Tony, and tell him about the fate of your car. And while you're at it, remind him of the ten telephone numbers. . . ."

"Listen, you bitch . . ."

But the woman had already hung up.

Quickly Tony dialed a number and his brother's groggy voice answered, "Hello . . ."

"Bruno, Tony. They just blew up my fucking car."

"What?"

"My Lamborghini. They just blew up my fucking hundred-and-fifty-mil car!"

"Who, for Chrissake?"

"I don't know who the hell who! Some broad. And what's this shit about ten telephone numbers?"

•   •   •

The house was cement block, one of a hundred or more just like it off the Monza motorway north of Milan.

There was nothing about the exterior to distinguish it from its neighbors. But the interior was all its own.

It served as a wire service and collection point for street dope dealers and gambling for all of northern Italy and a great deal of southern France.

They were waiting a block up the alley from the rear door of the building. Reela was behind the wheel with Carter in front beside her. Louis Corot was in the rear. Both of the men had Ingram machine pistols fitted with suppression silencers slung over their shoulders.

"There go the two wire men," Corot said as two men climbed into a small Fiat and drove away.

"Okay," Carter said, "three cars left. What have we got?"

Reela consulted the thick sheaf of typewritten pages Carter had gotten in Sicily. By now they had started calling the papers the "Zimbatti bible."

"Four. The guy who lives in the upstairs apartment. He's like an around-the-clock guard. The bookkeeper and two of the couriers. They're probably done counting by now. They'll most likely be sacking."

"Get ready," Carter said.

Reela started the car. Ten minutes later a man emerged carrying two sacks.

"That's one of the couriers," she said.

"Go!" Carter hissed.

The car was beside him before he knew it. And before he could react, two men wearing ski masks were prodding him with machine pistols.

"One twitch, little man, and you're dead," Carter growled.

"You two crazy? This is a Zimbatti layout."

"We know what it is. Knock on the door. Tell them you forgot your keys."

When the man didn't move at once, Corot prodded him toward the door.

"Crazy, you're crazy."

"Knock."

He did. A gutteral growl came from the other side. The man hesitated. Both Carter and Corot twisted the muzzles of the machine pistols into his sides.

"It's me, Santone. I forgot my fuckin' car keys."

As the door opened, Carter planted a shoulder in Santone's back. The man, moneybags still in hand, went sprawling on the floor inside. Carter and Corot were right behind him.

The surprise was complete. The second courier was just hefting two more loaded moneybags. The little bookkeeper, complete with green eyeshade, was closing his books to call it a night. The guard had opened the door. He stood by it now, his mouth gaping open.

The second courier was the first to understand. His hand disappeared under his coat.

"Don't touch it," Carter ordered. "If you do, I'll cut you in half. All of you, move into a line against the wall. Put your hands on your heads."

When they hesitated, Carter put a quick burst into a computer unit on a stand just to the left of the bookkeeper. The screen exploded, a few sparks flew, and the machine skittered across the floor until the plug was pulled from its outlet.

"Do it," Carter said.

"Against the wall, the position," Corot added.

All four men complied. Corot went down the line relieving them of their hardware. At the same time Carter moved to the desk. He took the two account books the bookkeeper had been working with and shoved them under his belt in the small of his back.

"Clean," Corot said, dropping the guns and knives he had collected into a wastebasket.

"Turn around," Carter barked. "Keep your hands on your heads and your legs spread. You, bookkeeper . . ."

"Bastard pricks," the man hissed.

"Aren't we all," Carter said dryly. "Where's the safe?"

"No safe," the man replied.

Carter sprayed the board floor inches from the man's feet. "Bullshit! Those four bags are the week's take. Somewhere you've kept out next week's operating capital."

"Over there, behind that mirror on the wall." The little bookkeeper was no hero.

"Open it."

He crossed the room and swung a large mirror outward. It turned on hinges and revealed a wall safe. The man reluctantly spun the dial back and forth until the heavy door of the safe clicked open. Carter emptied it while Corot kept watch on the four men.

The safe yielded a cashbox and a file of records. Carter thumbed through the records, shoved a few of them into his pockets, and pushed the rest aside. He picked up the box and grinned as he opened it.

Besides a great deal of cash it was stuffed with bearer bonds of large denominations.

Don Pepe's intelligence was right on the mark. The Zimbattis used the bearer bonds to get their profits out of the country and into Swiss banks.

Carter dumped the contents on the floor, tossed the box to the side, and again leveled his Ingram at the four men. "You know what to do."

"Yeah," Corot said, a look of disgust on his face.

The contents of the four large moneybags joined the pile on the floor. Corot liberally sprinkled the whole with a

squirt can of lighter fluid. Only when Corot took a cheap
lighter from his pocket did the four men gasp as one.

"What the hell . . . ?"

"You guys are nuts . . ."

"You do that, you won't hide anywhere in the world."

"That's millions . . . *millions* . . ."

Only the bookkeeper was quiet, staring at Carter's eyes
behind the ski mask.

The Killmaster shut them up with another burst into the
floor. "Burn it."

With a look of pain on his face Corot thumbed the
lighter and dropped it on the pile. The effect was one of
instant, whooshing flame, and in seconds the whole pile
was orange. It took only a few minutes and the pile of
money was smoldering ashes.

The courier, Santone, was actually crying. The other
three were stunned.

Carter spoke as he and Corot backed to the door. "Call
Bruno. Tell him everything that has happened here tonight,
and tell him to use the list of phone numbers tomorrow at
noon. Tell him that if he doesn't, tomorrow night will be
even worse. You got that?"

Silence, with all four of them staring in shock at the pile
of ashes.

"Bookkeeper!" Carter shouted. "You got that?"

"*Sì, sì, capisco.*"

Corot grabbed the wastebasket of hardware and they
were out the door. The doors of the car were barely shut
when the rear end of the sedan was fishtailing down the
alley.

Seconds later they were on the Monza highway with
Reela's foot on the floor.

In the back seat Corot was groaning. "Jesus, Jesus, all
that money . . ."

Carter laughed. "All for a good cause, Louis, all for a good cause."

"That's what you say."

"Do we still go after Pietro?" Reela asked.

"Oh, yeah," Carter said, checking his watch. "We should have just about enough time."

Pietro Zimbatti sighed with satisfaction. Already he had made love twice like a bull this night. And he knew that he would do it once more before he left.

He looked at the girl, Gabriella, as she sat on the edge of the bed brushing her hair. She was a whiner, a money-grubbing little tart. But God, what an enticing creature she was. She was unlike any of the others. With her, he felt like a master sculptor creating a magnificent work of art with the help of a model willing to follow his every direction. His every whim.

He had never experienced such abandon. Such freedom. Such a willingness to learn. Such a desire to please him. For the price of a car, a flat, and a huge allowance, of course.

He ran his hand down her dark, sheer gown. She was naked beneath it and the touch of her soft, silky skin immediately aroused his lust for the third time.

"No, Pietro, I'm tired," she whined.

"Yes," he said, pulling the gown down.

"No, dammit," she yelled as he put a hand over a breast. He began to massage it slowly, a circular motion, saw the color in her eyes deepen instantly. "No," she repeated, but her voice had gone breathy.

"Yes." He smiled down at her, continuing to rub. She formed the word *no* again with her lips and her head moved from side to side, protesting herself more than his hand. He let go of her wrist and put both hands on her breasts now. He rubbed slowly, saw her stomach draw in, push out.

"Goddamn, goddamn," she breathed. Her hands reached, clutched at him as he continued rubbing her breasts. "Do it," she gasped, "come on, do it."

His smile was cold triumph as he shed his robe, moved over her, felt her rise to him at once, spasmodic wildness enveloping her. He was rough with her, harsh, yet she stayed with him, begging for more and still more. She was something special, all right, something special, better than any of the others.

And then she screamed.

Pietro was yanked to his feet, and the girl, tape slapped over her mouth, was alongside him.

There were two of them, big men, with ski masks over their faces.

"What the hell do you think you're doing?"

"Shut up."

"You know who I am?"

One of them planted his fist in Pietro's belly clear to the wrist. He gasped, almost vomited, and fell to the floor.

They forced him to stand. His arms were placed around the girl's waist and his wrists were handcuffed together. The girl's wrists were handcuffed behind his waist.

Then they were being shoved down the back stairs of the apartment house and bundled into the back seat of a car. A woman was driving, but she had a scarf pulled forward over her face.

"What are you doing?"

"Taking you home, Pietro. Don't you always go home about four in the morning?"

"But I'm naked . . . she's naked."

"That's right, Pietro."

The girl blubbered behind her gag. Pietro Zimbatti cursed, pleaded, and did some whining on his own.

Eventually one of the men slapped a thick piece of tape over his mouth as well.

They drove along the bank of the Naviglio River and eventually turned off into the prosperous Alzaia Naviglio Grande section of the city.

Pietro now saw what they meant to do and sweat broke out all over his body. He tried to scream at them again when he saw the huge, familiar wrought-iron gate with his initials in gold leaf atop it.

Pietro and his mistress, still naked, were pulled from the car. One of Pietro's ankles was handcuffed to the girl's, then another set of cuffs bound his wrist to the iron grille of the gate.

"No, oh, dear Mother of God, no, not naked," he yelped, but no sound came through the gag.

One of the men leaned close to his ear. "Bruno is probably trying to call a family conference right now. When you see him, Pietro, remind him again about the ten telephone numbers. You'll do that, won't you?"

As the car drove away Pietro almost wished they had killed him.

It was almost dawn when the telephone rang beside the huge canopied bed. A thick arm came from beneath the quilt and patted the other side of the bed.

"Bastard, no-good bastard," the woman hissed in a voice that rasped like a file.

She rolled her heavy legs over the side of the bed and grunted her pasta-bloated body upright. When she reached her husband's side of the bed she yanked the phone from its cradle.

"*Sì.*"

"Signora Zimbatti?"

"*Sì, sì, sì . . .*"

"Your husband, Pietro, needs your help right away. He's at the front gate."

The line went dead.

Maria Zimbatti stared at the instrument for a moment, dropped it back on its cradle, and lumbered to the terrace windows. She threw open the tall windows and stepped out onto the terrace.

It was light now, with more than enough illumination to see the two bodies at the gate.

"Nudo," she whispered, and then started screaming curses down at her husband.

EIGHTEEN

It was chaos in the study of Bruno Zimbatti.

Pietro, his face flaming, paced the room, his arms waving wildly. "*Nudo*, they handcuffed the bitch and me together to my own gate . . ."

Antonio sat, his face in his hands. "My car. I'll kill the bastards!"

Carlo sat stone-faced, adding figures on a hand-held calculator. Now and then he would murmur a loud curse and slap the palm of his hand on the table before him.

Bruno was shouting into his private telephone. The moment he hung up, his brothers descended on the desk.

"Anything?" Pietro shouted.

"Two men and a woman," Carlo said, adding, "foreign —they should be easy to find."

"Shut up, all of you," Bruno said.

"It's the Sicilians," Antonio said. "It's Don Pepe, I know it!"

"Shut up!" Bruno yelled again, pounding the desk with his own fist. "It ain't Don Pepe. Carlo, how much gone from the country house?"

"Cash," Carlo replied, "about two hundred million. Probably another two hundred mil in the bearer bonds."

"There," Bruno said. "You think if Don Pepe does this, he's gonna burn four hundred million lire? Never! No, this is something we've never seen before. Whoever these people are, they got no rules we know about."

"Any of our people got a line on 'em?" Pietro asked.

"Nothing," Bruno replied. "They're trying to make us look like a bunch of idiots, and they're doing it."

"Well, what the hell are we going to do?" Antonio growled.

"For right now," Bruno said calmly, "we're gonna find out just what the hell they want."

He smoothed the paper containing the ten telephone numbers in front of him on the desk, and reached for the phone.

About a mile from the sprawling estate of Bruno Zimbatti, Louis Corot leaned back in a climbing belt and dug the climbing spurs deeper into the pole for comfort.

The digital circuit finder in his hand glowed. He dialed the number of the phone booth where Carter was waiting.

"Yeah?"

"I'm wired up to every phone coming out of the house," Corot said. "Your line will be open. It won't ring, it will just click. Keep them talking for at least two minutes."

"You're sure that thing will work?" Carter asked.

"I'm sure," Corot chuckled. "Once the call is completed, I can dial back in and tap every incoming and outgoing conversation on Bruno's hot line."

The digital face on the box in Corot's left hand began to read numbers.

"Here we go," he murmured. "Hang up and get ready!"

The telephone clicked. Carter flipped away his cigarette and closed the accordian door of the booth.

"Yes?"

Bruno Zimbatti's voice was a growl. "Who the hell are you?"

"It's not who we are, Bruno," Carter replied, "it's what we want."

"All right, all right, what the hell do you want?"

"You're bankrolling Drago Vain."

"I don't know what the hell—"

"Don't bullshit me, Bruno, I don't have time for it. Where's Vain?"

A long pause. "I don't know. He moves, all the time."

"But you can reach him." Another pause, shorter. "But you can reach him, for emergencies."

"Yes."

"Good," Carter said. "I want you to set up a meet."

"What the hell for?"

"Because you and your brothers are backing out of the deal, and I want Drago Vain."

"Just a minute."

Through Bruno's hand over the phone Carter could hear mumbled conversation. Then the man was back on the line.

"What's our guarantee that if we deliver Vain you'll get out of our hair?"

"My word, Bruno," Carter said with a harsh laugh. "What about it?"

Another short conference. "All right, I'll call you back in two hours."

"Just go through the list of numbers again, Bruno," Carter said, and hung up.

He waited a full minute and picked up the phone. "You on?"

"Yeah," Corot replied, and gave Carter the number of Bruno Zimbatti's private line.

It was the lunch hour, and the small trattoria near Milan's central telephone exchange was full of people, noise, and tobacco smoke.

A big girl with a pretty face, a deep bosom, and long hair sat in a rear booth. Nervously, she twisted a glass of wine, and almost jumped out of her skin when a leather-coated, corpulent man slid into the booth opposite her.

"You got them?" he said.

She nodded and slid a slip of paper across the table. "All ten of them are pay phones. The locations are there."

The man passed over an envelope with a smile. "You did good, Rosa. Now go back to work and forget everything."

The woman slid from the booth and practically ran to the door.

The corpulent man moved to a pay phone on the wall by the bar. He dialed, and Bruno Zimbatti's voice answered at once.

"Yeah?"

"I got all ten of 'em."

"Gimme," Bruno growled. "I'll get 'em covered."

Carter slouched behind the wheel of the car, his eyes scanning the street. He spotted all three of them the minute they moved into place. They weren't good. They stood like robots watching the telephone booth.

Carter started the car and slid from the parking space. He drove a mile across the city and slowed by a booth at the entrance to the Sforza Castle parking lot.

There were three of them here as well, in separate cars, their eyes glued to the booth. He checked two more locations before driving to the Hotel Leonardo da Vinci. Reela awaited him in the dining room.

"Well?"

"They got the numbers," Carter replied with a chuckle. "What shall we have for lunch? I'm famished."

An hour later, over espresso, Carter checked his watch.

He wrote Bruno Zimbatti's private number on a slip of paper and slid it across the table.

"Use the phone in the lobby."

Bruno grabbed the phone on the first ring. "Yeah?"

"Stupid, Bruno, very stupid. So you got the numbers. And we've got your number. One more lesson, tonight. We'll call again. In the meantime, Bruno, do yourself a favor. Hustle up Drago Vain."

The phone clicked. Bruno Zimbatti sat staring at the instrument in his hand.

"Well?"

"Did they get 'em?"

"Who is it?"

"Carlo," Bruno barked, "find that bastard Vain. I don't give a damn where he is!"

The Mundo Toy Company was located in a desolate area in the western suburbs of Milan. The dolls made here were shipped all over the world. Every fifth shipment into the port of New York contained heroin stuffed into the protruding bellies of organ grinders.

The office building fronted the factory itself behind a high chain link fence. Two uniformed security guards manned the front gate.

At five o'clock sharp, the factory workers filed out a rear gate that was closed and locked behind them. When this was done, the two guards on the rear gate entered the factory. There, in a small room, they monitored a television security system with cameras that constantly scanned the perimeter of the fence.

By five-thirty, only the four guards, the manager, Adolfo Camelli, and his secretary, Anita LaSala, were still on the premises.

Reela Zahedi, in a blond wig, slightly darkened eyeglasses, and a severely cut business suit, presented her card to the gate guards. She announced that she had an appointment with Signor Camelli.

She was buzzed through, and entered the office building.

Anita LaSala was a middle-aged woman with suspicious eyes. She accepted Reela's card and studied it.

"One moment," she said, and disappeared through the door behind her.

The card Reela had given the secretary presented her as the representative of a huge French toy distributor in Paris. The Mundo Toy Company didn't want or need any more French outlets, but it behooved the company manager not to turn away business blatantly. It might give the authorities a reason to question the company's activities.

Signor LaSala returned immediately with a frown on her face. Her boss would most likely talk to this woman for an hour, and she would be late for her dinner.

"Signore Camelli will see you. Right through there."

Camelli's office was a large barrackslike room with solid furniture, grimy, wire-meshed windows, and several old filing cabinets. A large, detailed map of Europe was thumbtacked to one wall. The man who got up from behind the desk was of average height, middle-aged and solidly built. His stiff, iron-gray hair was cut short, and although he was smiling politely, his flat gray eyes were as cold as two chips of granite. His fleshy face was as smooth and had the same flush as a baby's bottom.

He walked around the desk and held out a hand that was more suitable for handling a heavy truck's steering wheel than a pencil.

Reela ignored the hand and drew a silenced Beretta from her purse. "You have two choices, Signor Camelli: do as I say and live, or raise an alarm and die."

•   •   •

Fifteen minutes after Reela entered Camelli's office, a Volvo sedan pulled up at the front gate. On orders from the manager, the two men in the Volvo were admitted to the office.

Inside the office, they found the manager and the secretary sitting side by side on a sofa, shaking with fear.

Carter and Louis Corot barely paused. They moved on into the factory, through the warehouse sections, and into the video security area.

The two guards never had a chance. They were overpowered and handcuffed back-to-back before they realized they were under siege.

From the video room they were taken to a rear loading dock, where they were placed in a van with tape over their mouths.

"You take the right side, I'll take the left," Carter said.

For the next half hour they worked in tandem through the warehouse and factory. In all, they planted incendiary bombs with timers in twenty-three locations throughout the building.

This done, they returned to the main office.

"Signor Camelli, call the front gate guards on your intercom. Tell them to lock up the front gate and come in here at once."

The man had no choice.

The two guards, the manager, and the secretary joined their comrades in the van.

"Reela, you drive the van," Carter said. "Follow us."

Carter and Corot moved back through the warehouse and the factory, setting the timers. Minutes later they were on a secondary road north, with the van right behind them.

By the time the Mundo Toy Company erupted in flame, the van had been parked in the middle of a field and the Volvo was pulling up in front of the villa.

• • •

Bruno Zimbatti's hands were shaking and his lower lip was quivering when he put down the phone.

"What is it?" Carlo asked anxiously.

"Jesus, Bruno, you look sick," Pietro added.

"Mundo . . ."

"What about Mundo?" Antonio said.

"They burned it . . . they burned it to the ground."

"Jesus!" Carlo shouted. "A whole shipment, a whole damn shipment!"

The decanter of wine rattled against the glass as Bruno poured. "That's it, Carlo," he whispered. "No more. I don't care how much that deal with Vain is worth. We give the bastard away, that's it."

At precisely midnight, the telephone jangled on Bruno's desk. He looked at his three brothers and then picked it up.

"Yeah?"

"Talk to me, Bruno."

"Carlo set up a meet with Vain, tomorrow night."

"Where?"

"In Sardinia, our old family place, about thirty miles north of Cagliari."

"That's good, Bruno. Who's supposed to make the meet?"

"Carlo."

"You tell Carlo to be in Genoa tomorrow night, the lounge of the Excelsior Hotel. Alone, Bruno, at seven sharp."

"No fucking way. . ."

"Seven sharp, Bruno, and alone. If Carlo doesn't show, you know what goes up next? Your house, Bruno. And we don't give a shit if you're in it."

The line went dead and Bruno stared into space. The brothers shouted questions at him until, at last, he held up his hand for silence.

"Carlo, there's no problem, right? Vain don't know what's going on. He'll be there?"

"Sure, he'll be there. I told him nothin', like you said."

"Good, Carlo. Because you're going with them."

"Going with them?" the man cried. "Bruno, are you crazy? I'm not gonna put my ass—"

Bruno Zimbatti slapped his brother so hard his body made a complete turn before he fell to one knee.

"You're going with them, Carlo. And you'd better pray you got this Drago Vain in your pocket like you say you do."

NINETEEN

The ashtray in front of Carlo Zimbatti was practically full of cigarette butts. He was on his second drink. It was seven-thirty, and he had been jumping out of his skin every time someone came near him for the last half hour.

He was about to order a third drink, when a bellman appeared at his elbow. "Signor Zimbatti?"

"Yes."

"A phone call at the desk."

He had expected something like this. They wouldn't show themselves, not right away.

He tossed some bills on the bar and followed the bellman to the desk.

"This is Zimbatti," he murmured into the receiver.

"Drive to the Piazza San Matteo. Leave your car there and walk to the San Lorenzo monument."

"What then?"

"There is a phone booth across from the monument, at the head of the Via Connore." The line went dead.

Zimbatti exited the hotel, his hands sweating, his eyes searching. He had to look carefully, but he saw them, two of his best men a half block away in a taxi, one as the driver, and one in the rear.

Bruno had said alone.

Bullshit on that. Carlo meant to get them himself. He wasn't about to trot along without them for a meeting with Drago Vain.

Louis Corot stood in the darkened room above the square. Directly below him, the San Lorenzo monument shone dully in the spillover from two streetlights.

He watched as Carlo Zimbatti walked into the square. The man hesitated near the monument and then walked quickly around it.

Corot lifted a walkie-talkie to his lips. "Nick?"

"Yeah."

"He's here."

"Any sign of a tail?"

"Not yet. Wait . . . a taxi just pulled into a slot a block away and killed its lights."

"Could be something. Watch it," Carter growled. "Reela?"

"I'm ready, Nick."

"Okay," Carter said. "I'm making the call."

Corot kept the walkie-talkie on his lips. Zimbatti practically dived for the phone when it rang.

"All right," Corot said, "he's headed down the Via San Lorenzo toward the port. Nick, the taxi's moving."

"That's it," Carter said. "Everybody move!"

The taxi oozed behind Carlo Zimbatti, keeping a three-block distance. They paid no attention to a paint-streaked old Seat parked across the street a block away facing in their direction.

Inside the Seat, Carter waited, the motor idling. From low in the front seat he watched Zimbatti walk by. The

Killmaster smiled at the pinched look on the man's face

His eyes moved to the taxi as it neared. The driver was short, a small, squat figure behind the wheel. The one in the rear was sallow with pockmarked skin. Carter could see him clearly as he leaned over the seat.

The taxi was twenty feet away when Carter slid the little car into gear. He tromped the accelerator and braced himself against the steering wheel.

The driver of the taxi tried to veer away.

It was no good.

The Seat struck the taxi head-on, and Carter rolled out of the door. The driver was out cold, the windshield shattered where his head had collided against it.

The one in the rear was trying to unscramble himself from the floorboards. Carter opened the door and yanked him out by his ankles.

He heard the man scream and saw him try to reach into his jacket with his right hand. Carter kicked him in the elbow and then came down on his belly with both feet.

The man was writhing on the street as Carter sprinted away toward the flashing taillights of the Volvo.

Reela had the door open. Carter dived into the front seat and the rear tires screamed.

He came up and looked in the back. Carlo Zimbatti sat, his eyes flashing hatred, as Louis Corot ground the muzzle of a Beretta into his ear.

"Stupid, Carlo," the Killmaster growled low. "Very stupid."

The plane and pilot were the same duo that had flown them out of Greece. And just as before, the pilot saw nor heard nothing.

A black Mercedes sedan awaited them at the airport in Cagliari, Sardinia. Zimbatti was bundled into the rear between Carter and Corot. Reela drove.

A map was placed on Zimbatti's lap, and Carter held a penlight.

"You give directions, Carlo, and I want a complete layout of the old homestead. And if there's one tree out of place when we get there, you, my friend, are a dead man."

TWENTY

It was simple, but Carter knew it would be effective.

"She's your girlfriend, Carlo. She'll go in with you. You'll explain that she goes to Cyprus when the shooting is over. She'll be your contact there, your eyes and ears. That's why she has to be in on this meeting, close to you, very close. Got that?"

Zimbatti nodded mutely.

"Inside, you stall. You want everything clear to Vain. That's what this meeting is for. If Vain gets a hint that anything is wrong, you get it first."

Reela lifted a small Derringer from her purse. It had a huge bore. "It fires a single shotgun shell," she said with a smile.

"Be a good boy, Carlo, and you might live through this night," Carter said. "Take off, Reela."

Carter and Corot watched until the taillights disappeared and then they melted into the trees beside the road. They moved in a long arc, always toward the old compound, but wide of it. They came up two hundred yards behind the farm, and moved in from tree to tree.

"Go!" Carter whispered.

Corot moved on around the circle as quietly as a cat. If Carter knew Drago Vain, the bulk of his people would be on the outside, making sure no one could get to their leader.

When he was sure Louis Corot was in place, Carter moved forward again.

He heard the two guards seconds before he saw them patrolling, their machine pistols slung over their shoulders. One of them was smoking, and they stopped together to chat for a moment while he watched them. He saw them move apart again, noted carefully just how far each man went. He crawled forward, then waited again till their backs were turned, and slipped quickly around the corner of the house.

He waited, counting the paces, his stiletto ready.

In a moment, the first man passed him. He reached out with one hand for the collar of the jacket, and drove the knife deep into the neck with the other, pulling the body in quickly and lowering it silently to the ground.

He counted the paces again . . . seven of them now.

He heard the guard say casually, "Hey, Darby, where did you get to?" and he slipped out from under cover and threw himself along the ground. He rolled over and struck upward with the stiletto as he shot out a foot to trip his adversary and bring him down onto the blade.

He was on his feet again in a flash, dragging the two bodies quickly under cover. He looked up at the stars and knew that his stalk had taken twenty minutes.

He kept low as he moved around to the front. He met no other guards, and retraced his steps to the rear.

In the courtyard, he found Corot.

"Two on my side," Carter murmured.

"Same on my side," Corot said. "There's one on the roof in front."

"Leave him for now," Carter said. "Let's get inside."

"No," Corot said, "you go in from the rear. I'll back you up from the front, just in case."

Carter nodded and Corot moved into the shadows. The

rear of the house was dark, the only light coming from one side and the front.

His rubber soles made no sound. He appeared as a deeper shadow mounting the steps. The door was locked but easily picked.

Beyond it was a kitchen, old, with a stone fireplace occupying one corner. Carter crossed the stone floor and crouched in the doorway leading to a dimly lit hall.

Voices, low, to his right. He moved forward. He was nearly to the door when there was a shout and a loud blast.

Carter hit the door with his shoulder and it splintered inward. He rolled and came up with the Beretta in both hands.

The room was sparsely furnished, a few chairs and a single table. On the table was a kerosene lamp sending out a stark white pool of light. Directly beneath, in the pool of light and his own blood with half his chest blown away, was Carlo Zimbatti.

In a corner, in shadows, Carter saw two pairs of legs.

"Reela?" he called, hunkering against the wall out of the light.

Her voice, when it came, was gagging. "I shot the bastard, Nick."

"Carter? Is that you, Carter?"

"Yeah, Drago, it's me."

"You don't give up, do you, bastard."

"Not with assholes like you, I don't."

"I suppose my people outside are dead," Vain said.

The words were scarcely out of his mouth when there was the sound of Corot's Beretta and then the thud of a falling body.

"They are now," Carter growled, sliding his body to the right. The room erupted with sound, and a slug hit the wall a foot above his head.

"Can't see you, Carter, but I can hear you. Who you got on the outside. How many?"

"Enough."

Drago Vain laughed. "Enough? Maybe. But I've got the bitch. You must have really busted some balls to get Bruno to set this up."

"A few," Carter said. "Why don't you just hang it up, Drago? You're done."

"And what will you do, huh? Arrest me? Bullshit, Carter. You want my head. How many does he have outside, lady?"

There was a muffled curse and then a throttled scream as Vain did something to Reela to make her answer.

"One," Carter said, "there's one man out there."

"Call him in."

"No way," Carter replied.

"Call him in or I'll kill her," Vain growled.

"No, you won't," Carter said. "She's your only way out."

A chuckle. "You're right. God, you've been a pain in the ass, Carter. But then I suppose you always will be, until I kill you."

"Or I kill you, Drago."

"Yeah, one way or the other. I'm going out, Carter. Tell your man to shoot me or back off. He shoots me, I'll shoot her. Take your choice."

"Louis!" Carter yelled.

"Yeah!" came a shout from somewhere in the front yard.

"Back off. Vain's coming out."

"*Merde*," the other man hissed.

"Do it."

Carter saw the legs moving toward the door. He lifted the Beretta, but a shot was impossible. He couldn't tell where Reela's body ended and Vain's began.

"I'm going out," Vain said, "and she goes with me. And so do you. You'll take me out of this house, and you'll drive us to where I want to go. Then you can have her. A fair exchange . . . my life for hers. All right?"

Carter said nothing.

"You have to trust me," Vain said. "And you've won anyway. I concede that. Once I give you the woman, you can do what you like. But as far as she and I are concerned, this is a stalemate. If I live, she lives. You try to kill me, and she dies. Now, toss your gun forward and get into the light where I can see you."

"No," Carter said.

"Try to be rational," Vain said, and his voice was detached, cool. "I can't kill you today. I need you as much as you need the woman. But later I will kill you. I promise you. Now, put down your gun. Stick it forward where I can see it. I mean it, Carter. If you won't, I'll shoot the broad and take my chances."

Carter slid the Beretta across the floor.

"Good. Now call off your hound."

"Corot, we're coming out," Carter shouted. "Don't shoot!"

"Very good," Vain said, and pushed Reela forward to the door.

Carter stood up to meet them, and moved into the doorway, blocking their view of Corot.

"Take us out," Vain hissed, "or she'll suffer. And you will suffer after her. That wouldn't be as good as getting away, but it would be good enough." Suddenly the voice lost its detachment. "I'd enjoy that . . . making you watch what happens to her, then doing the same to you."

Carter opened the door and stepped through. He turned and backed away as Vain, holding Reela close to his body, followed.

The light was behind them now, illuminating them clearly.

"Reela . . . ?" Carter said.

"Yes," came the choked reply.

"Watch your heels on these steps."

"I'll try," she said.

"Damn," Vain chortled, "you're a reg'lar Sir Walter, ain't ya? Let's go, girlie . . ."

It was the last thing Drago Vain ever said.

Reela came down on the instep of his right foot with her right heel, a thousand pounds per square inch of painful power.

Carter dropped to his belly and reached forward in the same move. He grasped Reela's ankles and yanked her forward. She was only halfway down Vain's body when Louis Corot's Beretta exploded twice.

Carter looked up.

What was left of Vain's face showed intense astonishment. Then he turned and fell against the wall. As he slid downward, his face left a dark smear on the rocks.

The villa was located on a high cliff above the sea. Glass enclosed three-quarters of it on the Mediterranean side, providing a panoramic view that reached from San Remo, Italy, on the left, clear past Monaco, to the twinkling lights of Nice on the right.

The interior of the villa was an impressive montage highlighted by European art, French antique furniture, signed stained-glass windows, and imported Italian marble everywhere.

Carter guided Reela through a huge entryway into the villa's guest room. The party was in full swing. Laughter, the tinkling sound of ice in glasses, and muted music from a small band struck them like a wave from the sea.

Soft light seeped from hidden fixtures to filter through the rarefied air and illuminate fifty or sixty people.

In a quick pass around the room with his trained eyes, Carter spotted a very successful fashion designer, and the latest American tennis sensation. His partner was a petite redhead with mammoth breasts that seemed determined to escape her dress as she danced.

And in the far end of the room, languishing on a chaise, surrounded by a bevy of beauties, was Louis Corot.

He spotted Carter and Reela, bounced to his feet, and came over. "Nice little sublet, huh?"

Carter laughed and shook his head. "You'll spend every dime you made within a month, Louis."

"Ain't that how it's done, my friend?" the other man replied, and grinned.

Reela leaned forward and whispered. "Do any of these people know how you came into your wealth?"

"Hell, no," he roared. "I'm still in the 'antiquities' business down in Rome. Say, how about the scene in Milan?"

"What scene?" Carter said.

"You mean you haven't seen a paper?"

Carter and Reela exchanged looks. They had spent the last three days at the Hotel de Paris in Monaco . . . without leaving the bedroom.

"Or a television?" Corot added.

"No," Carter said. "What's up?"

"Come this way," Corot said, turning on his heel.

He led them down a long hall and into a study. He lifted a newspaper from the desktop and turned it toward them.

Carter scanned the story quickly. It didn't take long to digest. The previous evening, in Milan, three prominent businessmen had died in the fiery explosion of their limousine.

All Milan was discussing the deaths of the Zimbatti brothers . . . Bruno, Antonio, and Pietro.

In a way, Carter knew he had set it up by weakening them.

The old man, Don Pepe, in Sicily, had fulfilled his vendetta.

DON'T MISS THE NEXT NEW NICK CARTER SPY THRILLER

SINGAPORE SLING

Before heading for the old building, he had eaten his evening meal in a café run by an aged Chinese. The man had been attracted to an American who could speak his tongue.

"What brings you to our city, younger brother?" the ancient gentleman asked, keeping his eyes on his help while he rested his tired feet.

"I'm an architect back home. I spend my vacations looking at old buildings."

"We have many old buildings. What do you want to see?" the old man asked. He was small, very thin, but very bright. Nothing escaped him. He knew what was happening in every corner of his establishment while talking to the stranger.

"I design penal institutions back home."

The old man rolled his tongue around the literal translation. "I know not the word."

"Prisons. I design jails."

"Ah. We have many jails. Much theft. Too much dope trading. Bad. Very bad."

Carter smiled to himself at the hypocrisy. The old man was an opium user himself. He had all the signs. He even smelled of the last pipe he'd smoked. "I hear that drug smuggling is a hanging offense."

The old man was wary. As a user, he could be pulled in and sent to the scaffold. His only safety lay in the number of his people who were as addicted as he. The police could not take them all, so they left the users and went after the dealers. "You have heard right, younger brother," he finally said. "You look more like a policeman than an architect. How do I know you are not trying to trap an old man?"

"I have no traps, older brother. I simply observe. Where is the jail they keep the condemned?" He tossed in the question casually.

"Not many condemned right now. The dealers are lying low. If anyone is awaiting the hangman, he will be in the Justice Building." The old man smiled for the first time, revealing teeth blackened by the smoke of many pipes. They were mostly stumps, most uneven, some missing. The parchment skin of his face wrinkled as he went on. "Poor devils. What are they to do? We have used the powder and paste for hundreds of years. Smugglers are fourth and fifth generation. Are they to become fishermen or panderers?"

"I hear even foreigners are condemned to death," Carter added as he finished off the last of his coffee.

"I am told that two are in the basement cells of the Justice Building now," the old man said. He suddenly looked weary. A frown creased his ancient face. "But you will excuse me. Business is a tireless master."

That had been a couple of hours earlier. Carter had been watching the building since then. Police cars had brought in prisoners. He had seen no one leave who was not in uniform. It was late, too late for court appearances and the work of lawyers.

Carter had mulled over the situation carefully. He

couldn't go in blasting. The operation had to be as clean as he could make it. Howard Schmidt's latest invention rested on the seat beside him. The nerve gas was obviously the answer, but it, too, presented problems. He could hold his breath longer than most people, at least four minutes. That was all right for him, but what about the prisoners? How big were they? Could he carry them both out? He decided on a soft probe first.

Carter circled the building quietly. Fortunately, it stood alone with an empty lot between it and its neighbors on both sides. The weed-covered lots were being prepared for an expansion to the old building.

A small parking lot at the back held only three cars. A dim bulb shone over a small door, the only opening at the rear. Carter opened it a crack and peered down the length of a deserted hall.

With the agility of a night-stalking creature, he slipped inside and descended to the first basement, taking the narrow stairway two steps at a time.

"What are you doing . . . ?" a voice behind him started to say.

Carter swung without hesitation and chopped the lone guard on the side of the neck. The man went down hard. Carter dragged him to a door nearby and shoved him in among the brooms and mops. A mobile laundry hamper took up the rest of the space.

Carter found no cells on that floor, but he did find a small elevator at the end of the hall. There was no way he was going to use the elevator now, but it might be useful later.

He took the stairs to the next lower level, making a mental note of every detail as he went, including the venting system.

The second basement contained a group of small storage offices, a closet identical to the one on the floor above, and one long row of cells. A guard was watching television, his back to Carter.

The Killmaster crept up slowly, his black sneakers making no noise on the painted cement floor. He grasped the guard in a choke hold and held him immobile. Since most of the population was Chinese, he whispered in the man's ear in Mandarin, "Where are the two Americans?"

"I don't . . . understand," the man choked out in Cantonese.

Carter repeated the question in the guard's language.

"They are in the last cell to the right. They—" he started to say as Carter cut him off, rendering him unconscious.

The man from AXE deposited the unconscious guard in the closet directly below the one he'd used upstairs. The guard had no keys. Despite the decrepit appearance of the jail, all doors were controlled electronically from a control room.

He ran along the hall to the last cell. "Where is the control room?" he asked the two dejected Americans without preliminaries.

He must have looked like an apparition. "Hawk sent me," he hissed at them. "You know the layout of this place?"

"Part of the job," the smaller of the two said.

"Where the hell's the control room for the cell doors?"

"Main floor. Second door to the right."

"I'm going to take you out. Stay as close to the cell door as you can," Carter said, taking off at a run, not waiting for an answer. There was no point in telling them he might have to use the gas. He had the lay of the land now. He could handle it.

The two flights of stairs to the back door were scaled in seconds. He slipped around to the front, keeping to the shadows.

The cylinder would be useful after all. He took it from the car and clipped it to his belt. He unraveled a long thin wire from around his waist and attached a grappling hook that he unfolded from a pocketknife that resembled a Swedish army knife.

It took him two attempts and more noise than he intended before the small grappling hook caught and held. He donned gloves and pulled himself up the wire, hand over hand.

The roof was flat, A relatively modern rooftop air conditioner hummed quietly to one side. One of the two large fans alongside the unit was circulating air down below.

The simplest task was releasing the gas and leaving the cylinder propped up beside the air intake. The more difficult one was to get in and then escape detection while transporting two inert bodies.

Carter decided not to waste time trying to find a way in from the roof. He rappelled down the side of the building in seconds and was at the front door ready to move in when two officers entered in front of him, reporting for duty.

Too many variables, he said to himself. He hadn't checked on the time factors for the nerve gas. Schmidt said it would last for several hours, but how long would it take for it to take effect? He couldn't allow for people entering the building. His best bet was to get in fast, then use the elevator and the back door on his way out. He took two minutes to move his car to the rear parking lot, then glided, catlike, around to the front door.

No one was in sight. Carter took in several lungsful of air, expelling each, building up a high concentration of oxygen in his blood. Through long practice and the use of yoga techniques, he was capable of holding his breath for four minutes. Once, trapped in a submarine, fighting for his life, he had extended his limit to five minutes but had blacked out at that point. There was no way he could allow himself to black out today.

Carter crept in past the brightly lit front entrance and down the hall to the control room. On the way he passed the two officers he'd seen enter. They had made it only a few feet inside the door. He didn't stop. Every fraction of a second was precious.

Two men were slumped over the control panel. The panel's instructions were in German. The guards had duplicated them using Chinese characters. German was no problem for the Killmaster. He pulled the guards aside and found a switch that controlled the cells in the second basement and threw it. He left one of the guard's bodies drooped over it.

He took the elevator to the second basement. It was painfully slow. He checked his Rolex. A minute and a half had passed already. The door slid open to reveal two more guards on the floor, one toppled over on the other. Carter found the closet where he'd left the guard earlier, pulled out the laundry basket, a canvas affair with a metal frame over four sturdy casters, and wheeled it down the hall to the last cell.

Two and a half minutes.

As he worked, he thought the agents were an unlikely team, one so much smaller than the other, almost like a boy. He tossed the inert frame of the big man on the bottom and eased the smaller one on top of him. He covered them both with a soiled sheet, a precaution that was more prevention than necessity, and had them to the elevator before the third minute was up.

The elevator crawled to the main floor slowly. Carter was beginning to feel uncomfortable, small black and green spots floating before his eyes from time to time.

At last the elevator opened on the main floor. He pushed the cart toward the rear of the building, the casters playing tricks with him, the cart bouncing off the walls, first one side, then the other.

He came to the end of the hall and found a hallway crossing like a T. Which way? He turned left and soon found himself trapped at a dead end. Three times he had to stop and shove bodies out of the way.

Carter reversed his path and took the other end of the T. After twenty feet it turned sharply to the right and he was faced with a set of double doors. They were locked. He whipped out his Luger and shattered the lock. It took three rounds before the door gave way to a powerful kick from his right foot.

Four and a half minutes.

Carter was feeling the pressure build, threatening to pop his ears if he didn't release it. He exhaled, careful not to take in any of the gas. His vision was blurred and his actions slowed.

He reached the door and pushed the cart out into the night air just as his knees started to buckle. As the door closed behind them, he took a long breath, drawing the fresh air deep within his lungs.

He still wasn't out of danger. He struggled to his feet on rubbery knees and pushed the cart to his car. He opened the car door, threw aside the sheet, and lifted out the first AXE agent.

He had just placed the smaller body on the back seat when someone shouted from the other side of the lot. He grabbed for the other agent and had him half in the car when he felt two slugs tear into the flesh of his burden, followed by the sound of two shots.

Carter dropped the agent, whipped out his own gun, and crouched beside the car, offering as little target as possible.

Two officers appeared out of the darkness, their guns raised. The Killmaster dropped one with a leg shot. The other spun around and dropped, a 9mm bullet in one shoulder.

Carter kicked their guns to one side in the darkness as they lay moaning on the asphalt. He clubbed them senseless and left them to be found. There was no need to kill officers doing their duty, but he couldn't afford to be recognized or have them register the license of his car as he sped away.

The big agent was dead. Carter left him, with regrets, and scrambled into the car. Within seconds he was blocks from the Justice Building headed for the highway back to Singapore, two hundred miles away.

—from SINGAPORE SLING
A New Nick Carter Spy Thriller
From Jove in February 1990